Other Books by Jane Shand

The Darkling Duology
The Darkness Within Karas (Prequel novella)
The Shard
The Dark Cluster

Standalone
The Light Wielders

Newsletter Exclusive
Origin of The Fallen: The Crystal Mages
To claim this eBook use this link and sign up for my emails
https://www.janeshandauthor.com/contact

The Crystal Mages Trilogy
A Shimmer of Magic
A Glint of Blades
A Glitter of Power

The Fallen Mages
Legacy of the Fallen
Curse of the Fallen
Power of the Fallen
Return of the Fa'

JANE SHAND

PREQUEL TO THE DARKLING DUOLOGY

COPYRIGHT

Copyright © 2022 by Jane Shand

All rights reserved.

This is a work of fiction. All characters and events, other than those clearly in the public domain, are fictitious and any resemblance to actual persons, living or dead, or actual events is purely coincidental.

www.janeshandauthor.com

Cover design by Miblart.com

Dedicated to my family and friends.

Chapter One

I am going!" Rosa showed her prettiest pout and fisted her hands on her hips. Her father simply raised an eyebrow at her and returned his attention to the horse's hoof. Trust her father to be the one man in Virona who was immune to her charms.

"Papa, it has been two months since we heard anything. Something must have happened," she added, a pleading tone to her voice. This time it wasn't fake. Rosa's insides were in knots. Her brother would not stop writing to her. He had promised to keep in touch when he left for Karas. Besides, they were twins, and she could *feel* that something was amiss.

Rosa always knew when something was wrong with her brother. There had been one occasion when they were about eight, probably the age when she began to be rebellious, when she should have been doing her chores, but instead, she had run off to the beach to look for starfish and shrimp in the rock pools. Gianni had completed his chores and came to find her. Rosa heard him calling her name. She hid behind the rocks and hid her giggles behind her hand as Gianni ran past.

She played for a little longer and then the tide began to turn. She knew she must go home to face her father's punishment. She took three paces before she stopped. Something tugged at her. Gianni was in trouble! She didn't know how she knew it, but she didn't question it. It was no different to knowing when he was sick or upset even though he hadn't said. She turned back to the beach and began to run. She found him sprawled on the sand near some rocks. She had been drawn straight to him.

"Gianni! What happened?"

"It's my leg. Rosa you must go. Look, the tide is coming in. There is no reason for us both to drown."

"Don't be silly. You won't drown. The sea people would take you down to their lair and keep you for your amazing eyelashes."

Gianni grinned. "True. But that won't help you. They wouldn't want your annoying ways down there."

"I don't have to help you, you know." Rosa fisted her hands on her hips.

"Okay. I guess they might want you for your eyelashes too. They are nearly as long as mine."

Rosa chuckled. She had been examining Gianni while they teased each other. It seemed that he had dislodged a rock as he scrambled over them. It now trapped his ankle. He couldn't reach it because of the angle he lay at. It was quite large. She turned to regard the sea. It frothed and foamed around Gianni's wrists. There wasn't time to fetch their father. Her heart skipped a beat and then resumed at double pace.

"Well, maybe there is some good in having to lug all those horseshoes and bits of metal about. At least I will have the strength to move this rock," she spoke with utter conviction, though whether it was for Gianni's sake or her own, she couldn't have said. Rosa had been in so much trouble that day. Though she had saved Gianni and her father had praised her courage.

Rosa came back to the present as her father released the horse's hind foot with a deep sigh. The horse blew out a breath and he patted it absently.

"Karas is becoming a dangerous place, Rosa. I am not sure I wish to risk my daughter's life trying to chase up my son."

"I can look after myself, Papa. You know that."

Her father shook his head. "That could be the very thing that gets you in trouble. I have heard alarming things about their Dark Patrol."

Rosa tossed her curls and grinned. "They'd have to catch me first."

A smile tugged at her father's lips. But in his eyes, she could read the concern. For Gianni, and for her.

"Papa, I cannot sit here and do nothing. You don't need me for the work, and you can't leave work to go. It has to be me. We have no one else to send," Rosa looked down. Her hands were clasped tight before her. She released them and pushed them behind her skirts. Her father still stared, a deep crease between his brows. He crossed his beefy arms and bit at his lip.

"Isabel can come and cook for you," Rosa added slyly. Her father cleared his throat and turned away, though not before she saw the blush rising up his neck. It was about time her father found some companionship; it had been six years since her mother died. She liked Isabel with her free laugh and kind ways. No one could ever replace her mama, yet her father was not the sort of man to be left alone for so long.

When her father turned back to her, her heart skittered in her chest. She could see in his eyes that he was seriously considering letting her go. Part of her had not believed he would give his blessing. She had begun hoarding food and supplies in case she had to sneak away in the middle of the night. It had been exciting planning it, but now that it seemed she might actually go… She could admit to her trepidation. Though she hid the emotion well. If her father thought she was anxious, he might change his mind. Still, she was determined to leave, despite her fear.

"Very well. I know that if I try to stop you, you will simply sneak off one night."

Rosa opened her mouth to deny it and her father raised a hand.

"Do not try to deny it. I am not as dim or unobservant as you seem to believe." Rosa had the grace to dip her head as her father continued, "I noticed my best pack had gone and certain supplies and even the dried food." Her father wrapped an arm around her shoulders. She was tiny next to him. He made her feel safe. Was she really going to Karas without him?

"Come. I have some other supplies you should take."

Rosa followed her father back into the house that sat next to his farrier's shop. More recently he had been called upon to apply his blacksmith skills for other things. There had been some dispute that involved Virona's blacksmith. Rosa wasn't interested except that it brought in more work and thus more pay.

Inside the house her father encouraged her to fetch her supplies whilst he disappeared into his bedroom. When she returned he had something hidden behind his back. She couldn't help a flutter of excitement. What could he have for her?

With dramatic flair he brought the object to his front.

Rosa gasped. He held a dagger in a smooth leather sheath on a shiny new belt.

"Take it," he said, his voice a little hoarse.

With fingers that trembled, Rosa reached out and took hold of the belt and sheath. The dagger came free of its sheath with a gentle *shush*. The dagger gleamed and had a rose etched down the centre. She turned it over and over in her hands.

"It was supposed to be a birthday present. But you should have it now."

Rosa leaped to her father and threw her arms around him, careful not to skewer him with the bare dagger.

"It's beautiful, Papa! Did you make it yourself?" She released him to run a hand over the rose.

He nodded, a smile working onto his face. "It took a while. But yes." He shrugged. "People have been getting me to do more blacksmithing work since the argument with Lorenzo so I knew it would be easier to keep it a secret and the other work was good practise. You like it then?" he asked, running a hand through his dark, curly hair.

"I love it," she said softly. "Thank you."

After that they argued over what other supplies she might need, and he gave her a pouch of coins that she argued was too heavy.

"If you don't need them, you can bring them back. But if something has happened to Gianni, you might need to bribe some people."

By the next morning Rosa was ready to leave. Her father gave her the address that he had given Gianni. An acquaintance who lived on Main Street, where a lot of merchants had their businesses. Her father had hoped that Gianni would board with him until he found an apprenticeship. Gianni was exceptional with his hands. He could be a blacksmith, an artist, a potter, or work with cloth. Everyone that knew him had high hopes for his future.

The letters had come weekly for the first two months. Then they had stopped. There had been mention of meeting new friends and a new interest and scathing remarks aimed at the Assembly and the Dark Patrol. Then nothing.

Yet the Dark Patrol would have no reason to arrest Gianni. He hadn't a drop of magic in his blood. Rosa frowned as she stood with her father on the street, waiting for the cart that would take her away from everything she knew. Perhaps Gianni had made remarks in public against the Assembly and the regular guards had arrested him. Or the Dark Patrol's remit had widened.

She peered surreptitiously at her father who stood beside her with his arms behind his back. He appeared at first glance to be calm. But she could see the tiny flexing of his jaw and biceps. She had to keep her hands clasped to still their faint trembling. She told herself it was from excitement. She dropped a hand to the hilt of her beautiful new dagger. Could she use it, draw blood, if it came to it? She swallowed hard. She had always got by on wit, determination, and pretty dimples mostly. She had no idea if any of that would help her in Karas. Still, she could think on her feet, and she was confident she would find a way. Besides, Gianni was her twin, her other half, and she missed him. Something wasn't right so she had no choice.

Her attention was yanked back to the street as a rumble announced the arrival of the cart. It was one of many that regularly carried goods to the city four days to the north. There were a couple of inns on the route, though the first two nights would be spent bedded down outside around a campfire. Her father had chosen Signor Edoardo to take her to Karas. He was well known to everyone and a gentle soul. He climbed down from his seat to help Rosa up with her belongings, then he waited to the side whilst her father nearly squashed her with his hug. Her eyes prickled, but she managed to keep her tears in check.

"Be careful, you hear? Don't use your magic unless your life depends on it," her father admonished her. He stared deep into her eyes, and she feared that he was about to tell her she couldn't leave, she was too young. Instead, he sighed. "And if you can't find anything after a week, come home. We'll get the law involved then." Her father stared into her eyes until she nodded. He pressed his lips to her forehead and then lifted her, as if she weighed nothing, onto the seat at the front. Signor Edoardo clambered up beside her.

"She'll be all right with me," Edoardo declared, then he clucked to the horses, and they were off. Rosa peered back over her shoulder until her father passed out of sight beyond a turn in the road. She swallowed and firmed her jaw. She was really doing this. She would find her brother and either help with his problem or bring him home. From the corner of her eye, she saw Edoardo briefly look at her. But he turned away without speaking.

Chapter Two

Rosa stared wide-eyed as Karas drew ever closer. Her heart tripped along inside her chest. But it was at least half with excitement. She was also looking forward to a decent bed. Sleeping out under the stars had not been fun. She was certain she had managed to lay her blankets on the stoniest area in the whole campsite both nights. She had tossed and turned for most of those nights. The two nights since had at least been at inns. Although they had hardly been salubrious. She grudgingly admitted to herself that she was soft. This was going to be harder than she had thought.

"I'll set you down here, signorina." Edoardo pulled the cart off to the side of the road.

Rosa turned back to him. "You aren't coming in with me?" She couldn't quite keep the anxiety from her voice.

Edoardo cleared his throat and looked everywhere except at her. "I'm sorry, signorina. But I have no business in Karas. Your father paid me to bring you to Karas, is all. If you need to leave, there will always be carts coming back this way. Your father's friend'll know how to contact one of 'em."

Edoardo stepped down from the cart and made his way around to her side. She passed him her pack and then accepted his hand to help her down.

"Thank you, Edoardo," she said softly.

He bobbed his head and clambered back up into the cart. "Good luck, signorina," he said with a brief nod. He clicked his tongue and turned the horse and cart around. Rosa blinked as it began to trundle away from her. A hollow opened in her stomach. She was alone. Then she straightened her shoulders. She was Rosa and she was resourceful, and she had a mission. She dug out the address her father had given her, slung the pack over her shoulders and strode towards the city gate.

The guard gave her piece of paper only the most cursory glance before admitting her. It seemed as long as you appeared to have a reason for being here, that was all the guards cared about. The throng of humanity within the open area beyond the gate was intimidating. But they were not interested in her. Slowly they moved off into the city and dispersed. Her father had written directions from the gate to Main Street onto the same piece of paper and she checked them again before setting off with a determined stride.

Rosa gawked at the rows upon rows of buildings. At the temples that sat at every crossroads. Each one a different size and shape. Though every temple except the Temples of Enara were square. When she saw the first round temple she stopped and stared. A woman in a flowing dress with a flawless face saw her and said a blessing over her. Embarrassed, Rosa moved on. She stared in wonder at the mass of people all with somewhere to be. It was so much busier than Virona, a place where nothing much happened. This was the place to be! It had a thrilling energy to it. *You are here for a purpose*, she admonished herself. Though once she had rescued Gianni from whatever mess he had got himself into, she would be back.

The scent of mud and decay announced the river before she saw it. It flowed murkily towards the harbour which lay well out of her sight. Ahead of her was an arched bridge. Beneath it ragged men and boys sat with fishing rods dangling into the water. She wouldn't want to eat what came out of that water. But she supposed some people had no choice. Her thoughts immediately turned to the fat coin pouch tucked away in a hidden pocket of her petticoats. One of the many rumours that had reached Virona was of the corruption now rife within the Assembly. A corruption that allowed the rich to become richer and the poor to become poorer. Crime was also on the increase. Rosa shook her head. None of that was her business. She needed to stay focussed on her mission.

Once across the bridge she soon reached more upmarket neighbourhoods. It wasn't far to Main Street now.

Main Street bustled with activity. No doubt in the hotter afternoons it would be quieter. Certainly, in Virona everyone tried to complete as much business in the mornings as possible. Stalls with bright awnings lined the edges. The stall holders shouted to compete with their neighbours. Rosa's senses were assailed by clashing scents. Spices tickled her nose and were joined by tallow and the earthy scent of vegetables and fruit. Ladies sent their servants to haggle with the stall holders for the best price. This street was still the centre of commerce for the city. Though the Assembly Headquarters had relocated to another building outside the city almost twenty-five years ago, people still came here for their produce.

There were some signs of a slow decline, however. Rosa noted one half-empty shop and a gap among the stalls lining the street. Rosa's father said that the newer Merchant Street was vying with Main Street to become the place to shop if you were a wealthy woman. So far, it had not tempted all the wealth away. Rosa eyed some of the ladies strolling along the street. She glanced down at herself and pouted. She needed to spend some coin on a couple of new outfits. Virona was obviously behind the times when it came to fashion. Even though the dress she wore was pretty and flattered her petite, yet curvy figure, it would not do. The lines of it were wrong. Naturally her father wouldn't have had any clue about this. And probably would have been baffled if she had brought up the subject. Maybe she should have spoken with Isabel. She was a woman. Surely, she would have understood. Rosa sighed. Too late now.

Rosa ploughed on, trying hard not be distracted by the glitter of jewellery or the flash of rainbow fabrics. She had somewhere to be. She passed the squat, functional building that was once the Assembly Headquarters. Now it announced itself as the Records Office. Like the temples, it had its own open area around it. Unlike the temples, no one was entering or leaving. Whatever was recorded in there, no one was interested.

No one was sure why the Assembly had moved. It appeared to be a huge secret. Though people had speculated: mould, rats, ghosts. Too easy a target for the Resistance. She plodded on along the street. The stalls ended and the buildings became residential. Window boxes hung at many windows, narrow balconies allowed windows to be opened wide and potted plants sat on doorsteps. Rosa glanced at her piece of paper. She was looking for number 35. Her father's friend owned the whole house. He had a wife and two daughters, though they were both older than Rosa. One was married, but the other still lived at home.

Rosa found she was more nervous to meet the daughter than the father. She located number 35 and with a deep breath stepped up to the door and rapped the brass knocker. She gratefully dumped her bags on the doorstep, wishing she had thought to catch a ride in a carriage, although she had no idea how one did that in Karas. The knocker thudded against the door. It was too thick to hear any approaching footsteps from within, but moments later the door opened, and a tall, thin man peered down at her disdainfully.

"Yes?" he asked impatiently.

Rosa swallowed. "I am Rosa d'Alessi. Gianni's sister. I have come searching for him. My father sent me here…" Rosa's voice trailed off under the cool stare of the man. He was dressed well, but he was not Marco Fiscella, the merchant who was a friend of her father. They had met on many occasions when Marco had been brought to Virona by his father on business. Rosa thought they had been big in cheese in those days. But she had not paid much attention to that part of her father's tales. Marco had bumped into her father one day and they had played together. Later Marco's father had brought them for new horseshoes and the friendship had been sealed.

"Please wait here," the man shut the door in Rosa's face. She bit her lip and scrunched the paper in her hands. What would she do if Marco wouldn't let her in? She pulled her brows down. She would make a scene.

The door opened once more. "Please come in Signorina Rosa." This time the servant's voice was less cool, though he still appeared rather haughty.

Rosa stepped forward and made to grab her bags. The servant tutted at her and lifted them himself. Rosa felt her cheeks warm as she entered the Fiscella house.

Chapter Three

Rosa tried hard not to stare as she entered the large entrance hall. Half of her own house would have fitted within it. The floor was of shiny tiles of various shades of blue. It formed a restful pattern. Large pots of the deepest blue sat to either side of a sweeping staircase and tall orchids spilled over the lip of the vases, perfuming the air with exotic scents. She was not given long to admire the hall as the servant indicated, with a jerky motion, towards a door on the left. He knocked, opened the door and announced in his deep voice, "Signorina Rosa, sir."

He imperiously waved Rosa towards the door. She looked back at her bags, sat beside the front door, and then squared her shoulders before entering the room. The room was a study or office. It was all wood panelling, brown leather and the dusty smell of books and ledgers. An empty fireplace sat to one side and standing before this was a man of middle years. He turned as she entered and regarded her with keen interest.

Rosa bobbed her head. "Signor Fiscella?"

The man smiled at her and waved a hand. "Please, your father and I are good friends, please call me Marco."

Rosa gave him her best smile. "Then you must call me Rosa," she said coyly. She saw him respond to that look, as most men did. She was fully aware of what her looks did to most men. She had big, dark eyes that her friend Alessia described as 'pools of melted chocolate every man wanted to swim in'. She had once also threatened to kill Rosa and steal her long lashes. They had rolled around the floor in fits of giggles over that. She had an abundance of black curls that framed a heart shaped face and though she was petite, she had curves in all the expected places.

Marco's expression turned wry and the look he bestowed on her next was that of an indulgent uncle. He had his own daughters; he would understand their ways.

"So, to what do I owe this pleasure? I am honoured to have been chosen to host both the d'Alessi children, but your father asked me to help find an apprenticeship for Gianni…" Marco's gaze became questioning.

"Is Gianni still here?" Rosa asked eagerly. She knew in her heart he was not, yet she still had to ask.

Marco frowned uncertainly. "No. He left my house to take up new accommodation a month or so ago. He had an apprenticeship arranged with a master potter and artist. Were you not aware of this?" Now his eyes showed concern.

Rosa shook her head. "We have not heard from him at all in that time. He did not mention that he had found an apprenticeship. The last we knew, he was still living here.

Then nothing. My father eventually agreed to let me come and find him."

Marco's frown deepened. "Surely, it would have been better to send," he paused as his gaze took in her petite form, "a trusted man. Or even to write to me for information. Forgive me, it seems a little reckless to send a young girl, alone, to this city."

Rosa lifted her chin defiantly. "I am certain that my brother must have got himself into some trouble if he has not written. There were no *trusted men* to send. Besides, I am not without my own resources." Rosa placed a special emphasis on the word 'resources' and she saw Marco's eyes widen as he realised what she meant. Marco strode to the window and peered out as if he feared the Dark Patrol might already be striding up the rode to arrest him.

"You must not speak of such things! And by all the gods and goddesses, do not use those 'resources'," Marco hissed at her.

"I have no intention to, unless it becomes necessary," Rosa said. "I may be young, but I am not an idiot."

Marco's posture relaxed and he chuckled. "No, if you are related to Dario, you would certainly not be an idiot." He sighed. "I am sorry. The Dark Patrol have begun gathering up any and all users of … resources. It is a very dangerous and volatile time for a young lady to wander around on her own." He shook his head. "When your brother moved out, I assumed he had informed you. He seemed excited at his prospects. I cannot imagine why he has not written to you. Perhaps the letters are simply delayed."

"It has been weeks. We are twins; I can tell when he is in trouble." Rosa shrugged, not sure if Marco would believe this. Many scoffed when she spoke of the bond between her and Gianni, but she knew different.

She could remember many occasions when she had known things about Gianni without having to be told. One of the first had happened when she was about six. Gianni had behaved as normal, and he looked normal. Her father had not noticed anything was wrong, but Rosa *knew* that his stomach wasn't right.

"Why haven't you told Papa that you have sickness in your tummy?" Rosa demanded of Gianni.

"I don't feel sick!" he replied defiantly.

She raised a delicate eyebrow and pouted. Even at six she had a very good pout.

"Fine. I do feel a bit sick. But if I tell Papa, he will make us all stay here, and I want to go to the fair!"

"Oh. I forgot about the fair. It wouldn't be right that we all miss out just because you feel sick. I won't say anything if you don't!" Rosa grinned.

Gianni had thrown up at the fair and they had returned home early. But at least they had gone and seen the jugglers and the dancers.

There had been other times when he fancied a girl, or someone had upset him and she knew, even though she had not been there, and before he spoke. It worked the other way round too. Gianni often guessed things about her. Though not as often.

Rosa smiled to herself. But perhaps it was not a twin thing and had more to do with the fact she had magic. It was such a shame that Karas had taken against magic-users.

Whatever had occurred here twenty-five years ago had a lot to answer for. There were many rumours around a night with strange lights up on the headland where the Assembly had their research facility, now the new Headquarters. But the Assembly had hushed it up and ten years later they set up a new elite guard. The Dark Patrol. That was when persecution against magic-users in the city began. It was also when other rumours began to spread. Rumours of terrible things happening to some children with magic. Rosa couldn't help the trickle of ice down her spine. It could have happened to her. Now, though, she was too old. Once you were over the age of fourteen, your magic settled and stabilised. Nothing could warp the nature of your magic then.

"I was surprised when I did not hear any news from Gianni. I had thought we were on good terms when he was here. But I supposed he was too busy with his new work, and I was rather busy too. If I had thought for an instant that he might be in trouble…"

"It is not your fault. You had no reason to think it. Either something happened after he moved, or he lied to you. It was very good of you to take him in. It certainly wasn't your responsibility to check up on him."

Marco raised one eyebrow. "I believe I should have done more. Your father entrusted his son to me. I should have checked on his apprenticeship. But he certainly came across as a fine and honest young man." Marco pursed his lips.

"He is. But if he felt that lying would help you in some way – keep you out of danger, perhaps – then he would not have hesitated," Rosa said ruefully. He had done the same for her on more than one occasion. She had been the one to push boundaries as they grew up. He had taken the blame for a few things that she had done to save her from punishment. Though only when she was already in her father's bad books.

Signor Fiscella promised that in the afternoon he would take her to the address that Gianni had provided for his apprenticeship. Rosa hoped it was real for so many reasons. Not least of all because she would be very disappointed if he had lied to Signor Fiscella after he had taken him in, fed him and helped him as much as such a busy man was able. Also, if he had begun an apprenticeship or at least meant to, it would give her one more clue. She found herself desperately hoping that she would walk in, and Gianni would be there, all smiles and sheepish looks and apologies for not writing. A hollow feeling behind her ribs told her that was not likely.

"So, how is your father these days?" Marco asked, breaking into her gloomy thoughts.

"He is well. He does well enough from his farrier work and now he has been asked to do blacksmithing. There is some dispute with the blacksmith." Rosa shrugged. She wasn't interested in the stupid feuds between supposed adult men. But she knew the extra money would be welcome. "He has a girlfriend too," she grinned. "He would be horrified if he knew I had called her that. But she is good for him."

Marco nodded and stared off into the distance. "I liked your mother very much. She was good for Dario too. You wouldn't remember, but I came to her funeral." Marco's smile was wistful. "You and Gianni have certainly grown a lot since then. How old were you? Five?"

"Four," Rosa replied. Her memories of her mother were dim but happy. She remembered smiles and hugs and a gentle perfume. A slender woman with dark eyes and a ready laugh.

"Well, we must certainly do what we can to find your errant brother. I wouldn't want to disappoint Dario. He is a big man too; I wouldn't wish to make him angry either!" Marco chuckled, but there was a hint of a frown on his forehead.

"If my brother has lied to you and got himself into trouble, there will be no blame towards you. It'll be Gianni facing Papa's wrath."

Marco nodded absently. "Still, I do feel responsible. He was under *my* roof. I agreed to look after him and it appears I have done a poor job of it."

There was nothing Rosa could say to that. Marco was a good man. Gianni would owe him an apology no matter what had happened.

⁓ ∾ ⁓

Rosa was given a room of her own. It had a view out into the Fiscella gardens. They were well tended and full of splashes of bright colour and citrus trees. When she managed to open the window, she was met by heady fragrances wafting up from the flowers. A bath was drawn for her and then she was invited to join the family for a light lunch.

Signora Fiscella was a slightly plump lady with a beaming smile and her hair in a neat bun.

"Please call me Sophia," she insisted, kissing Rosa on both cheeks. "We are so pleased to be able to have you here."

Rosa dipped her head and thanked her graciously. The welcome of Carlotta, the daughter, was more studied. She was polite enough, but her expressions were reserved. Rosa treated her no differently to her mother. She had no wish to upset the family. Besides, she might need her help at some point. Rosa hid her grin as an idea came to her. They usually did.

"Carlotta, I am certain that you must know far more than me of suitable fashion for the big city. Virona is a bit of a backwater and I fear that I must look very out of place. I had hoped that you might be able to steer me in the right direction to buy a couple of proper dresses." Rosa kept her gaze down demurely, but eyed Carlotta surreptitiously. Carlotta was a few years older than Rosa, though five years younger than her married sister. To be looked up to must be a novel thing. She had inherited the more austere looks of her father and was no great beauty, but she was attractive, and her face was full of character. Rosa thought that they might become friends. At Rosa's words her eyes brightened, and her lips curved up in a genuine smile. She sat up straighter in her chair.

"I would be delighted to help you, Rosa," she declared. Her gaze turned critical. "Indeed, I believe we should go shopping before you visit this man your brother said he was apprenticed to. You want to make the right impression." She turned beseeching eyes on her father. "May we go shopping first, Papa?"

Rosa hid her own smile. The eyes and the tiniest hint of pleading in her voice were just how she spoke to her father. Would it work better on Marco than it did on her own father?

Marco regarded both girls with slightly narrowed eyes. "You are certain this is necessary? The dress Rosa wears looks entirely suitable to me."

Carlotta made a tsking sound. "Papa, you know nothing of women's fashion. Everyone will know she has come from some backwards town, and she will draw all sorts of the wrong kind of attention, like an orange on the tomato stall. She is here to make discreet enquiries; she should blend in. Tell him, Mama!" Carlotta turned to her mother to enlist her help.

Sophia laughed good naturedly. "Well, you are right that your father has little knowledge of women's fashion. And perhaps blending in would help with Rosa's endeavours."

Marco threw up his hands. "I am outnumbered. If this is necessary then by all means, go shopping. If you are home early enough, we might still pay a visit to Signor Rossi."

After that Rosa and Carlotta discussed colours and the latest trends in Karas over cheese, fruit and bread. There was also a delightful, sweet drink that was made from the lemons in their garden. It had been cooled by leaving it in a covered hole beneath the pantry floor. They kept a number of items in there that needed to remain cool. Rosa decided she would inform her father he must dig a hole so that they could have cool drinks. She smirked to herself as she imagined the look on his face.

Chapter Four

Rosa struggled up the stairs of the Fiscella house with her purchases, Carlotta giggling behind her. Rosa had enjoyed her time with the woman. It had been like having an older sister. No one could replace her best friend Alessia, yet it was nice to have another friend, even for just a while. For most of her life it had been just her and Gianni for most of each day. But now he had moved on.

Rosa dumped her bags inside the room she had been given for the duration of her stay. While she had been shopping, she had been able to push aside thoughts of Gianni. She had always known that one day he would leave to find a career and she would be left alone. Part of her missing. She had felt stuck in Virona and simply drifted without purpose. Perhaps she would find it here in Karas. She freshened up and then drew out the pale blue dress that Carlotta had persuaded her to buy first. It was delightful and so in fashion. Someone knocked on her door.

"Come in," she called.

Carlotta entered and a grin broke out on her face as she took in Rosa. "Oh! Yes, I knew that one was for you the instant I saw it. Look." She drew Rosa to the wardrobe and swung open the left-hand door. Rosa gasped. Hanging on the back of the door was a large mirror. It was the largest and clearest mirror she had ever seen.

"It must have cost a fortune!" she whispered, reaching out a hand to touch it.

"Papa knows the man that makes them. I think he received rather a decent discount," Carlotta said. "But never mind that! You are supposed to be admiring the dress."

Dutifully Rosa stepped back and did a twirl. Carlotta had indeed been right to insist. The dress was exactly to fashion and complimented both her figure and her colouring. She grinned across at Carlotta. "A wonderful afternoon of shopping and we were back in time for me to visit the pottery maker, Signor Rossi. We make a good team."

Carlotta's smile turned wistful. "Yes, we do. I don't have many friends in Karas. Too much politics involved between this merchant and that. You are always wondering what's behind the friendship. What are their parents hoping to gain from it? It puts a strain on the friendship." Carlotta shrugged awkwardly. "But there is nothing like that with you."

"Perhaps I can come back and visit, once I have located my errant brother. Or you could come and visit the backwards town of Virona." Rosa grinned. She knew why Carlotta had used that phrase; it had been to add weight to her arguments for a shopping trip. Carlotta grinned back conspiratorially.

Rosa was summoned downstairs where Marco waited.

"I have a small carriage waiting to take us to Signor Rossi." He eyed Rosa critically, much as Carlotta had earlier. Then his lips curved. "It seems your shopping trip was successful. I imagine everyone in Karas society will consider you one of them, now. Even if they didn't before," he said gallantly.

Rosa gave him a curtsy and then followed him outside to the waiting carriage. It was an open carriage pulled by a white horse. The coachman was dressed in a smart dark-blue livery. The seats were red velvet and there were a number of plump cushions for added comfort. Marco handed her up before stepping up himself and telling the coachman where to take them.

Rosa sat with her hands clasped on her knees in silence. Marco shot her glances from time to time but for a few minutes he didn't speak. Rosa watched as they turned off Main Street and clipped along another residential street. They made a few more turns and she was soon entirely lost.

"The city is quite large, and it takes a long time to find your bearings. If at any point you need to find your way around, head to a temple and ask there. The priests and priestesses are duty bound to help, and there is a temple of some description on most crossroads." Marco gave her a reassuring smile; he must have seen some of her bewilderment on her face.

"Thank you. That is good to know. I hope we turn up at Signor Rossi's and my scoundrel brother is there and it has all been a misunderstanding."

"But you do not believe that, do you?" Marco asked.

Rosa shook her head, her black curls caressing her cheeks as she did. "No. I think he will have got involved in something that he shouldn't. I just hope he hasn't been arrested."

Marco cleared his throat. "Does he, er, have *resource*s?"

Rosa smiled wryly. "No. My mother did, and I inherited it. But not Gianni. For which I got no peace once it became known. I think that might also be a driving force behind him wanting to do something, anything, to prove himself in some way."

Marco nodded thoughtfully. "When we are in private once more, I would be interested to know its nature."

Rosa turned wide eyes on him. He had seemed so anxious for her to not speak of it earlier.

He caught her look. "I can't help my curiosity. It lands me in trouble sometimes."

After a time, they entered a street bursting with pink flowered bushes that poured perfume into the air. Oleander.

"This street is named for the bushes. Signor Rossi has a shop and studio with apartments above at the far end of the street," Marco pointed along it. This was a street for the wealthy to live as much as Main Street was. "He is expecting us, so he will not be with a customer."

Rosa swallowed in a dry throat. She had to forcibly relax her hands that wished to clench the material of her new dress. She couldn't allow that. It had not been cheap. And she wanted to come across to this Rossi as poised and in control. Older and wiser than her mere sixteen actual years.

The carriage pulled over and Marco helped her down. He asked the carriage to wait. The shop had a large glass window at the front, the largest shop window Rosa had ever seen. It was made from a number of panels of glass held together by dark wood. No one could make a single pane of glass that big. The shop sign announced, 'Rossi Ware' and the window displayed some arresting pots, vases, cups, teapots and plates. The colours were vibrant and the painting exquisite. Her brother could do a lot worse than apprentice with this man.

Marco called her gently and she drew her attention back to him. He pushed open the front door which caused a bell to tinkle overhead. He held it open for her to enter. The interior was well lit by oil lamps on every wall and smelled earthy. The dense odours of paint and clay. A man sat behind a desk marking something in a ledger. He looked up as they entered and smiled warmly at Marco.

"Marco! It has been too long." He stood and came over to them, giving Marco a pat on his shoulder. He was a slender man in brown with a paint-stained apron over the top. He turned his gaze to Rosa and his eyes lit. "And who is this delightful young creature?" His eyes began to roam up and down her body, and Rosa felt colour flush into her cheeks at his presumption.

"You, you would make an exceptional model."

Rosa realised he had been examining her in the same way he would an exotic flower arrangement. She felt foolish for assuming a different kind of interest.

"May I introduce Signorina Rosa d'Alessi. Gianni's sister."

Signor Rossi squinted. "Gianni? That name rings a bell." His expression cleared. "Oh yes, he came here asking for an apprenticeship. He showed me his work. It showed great promise and skill. I was sad to have to turn him down."

Rosa's stomach lurched downwards. She had known; still, it was different hearing it out loud. Before she could speak, someone else entered the room from the back.

"Signor Rossi … I am sorry, I didn't realise you had customers."

A young girl stood in the doorway. She too wore an apron, though hers had fewer stains. She couldn't be any older than Rosa herself, perhaps even younger. She was taller than most women Rosa had seen, which was deceptive. She was also pale of skin. But it was her hair and eyes that drew her attention most. Her eyes were the pale blue of a winter sky and her hair reminded Rosa of the caramel treats that Isabel sometimes made.

"No. No. Come through, Valetta. This is Signor Fiscella and Signorina d'Alessi. They are not here as customers." Signor Rossi tilted his head in query. "Why are you here? Your note didn't mention the important reason."

"My brother, Gianni, has gone missing, Signor. But not until after telling people that he was working for you," Rosa blurted. She hadn't meant to be so blunt, but the weight of it was unbearable. If he hadn't come here, where was he? How was she to find him when the trail had already gone cold?

Rosa noticed the sudden spark of interest in the girl's eyes which she quickly hid.

"I cannot imagine why your brother would give such an impression. I would have taken him on if not for Valetta here. She is my apprentice and I only have room for one." Signor Rossi smiled at the girl, who dipped her head shyly. "She is also a fantastic athlete and I fear I may lose her to the lure of competing before long. She won the short sprint annual competition last month. Beating all the women from the whole country!" Rossi sounded proud enough to be her own father. "I am very sorry that your brother is missing. But I am afraid I really cannot help you find him. Unless he has taken an apprenticeship with another potter and mixed up our names? I will ask around. I wished that I could have taken him on as well as Valetta here. He was very skilled."

Marco and Rossi chatted, and Rosa half listened as she drifted away.

"My wife, Sophia adores the last piece you did for us. She would love to commission another vase. A big one for orchids. I don't know where we will find room, but if she wants this, she shall have it. She rarely asks me for anything, so I cannot refuse her."

Rosa smiled to herself. It seemed Marco was a generous and romantic man. It was a shame he didn't have a son of similar age to her… Rosa caught herself daydreaming about boys and romance. She had better things to think about! Especially as the boy in her dream had a remarkable resemblance to Signor Fiscella! She turned all her attention towards the nearest pot. From the corner of her eyes, she saw that Valetta, the apprentice, had not left the shop yet. She was watching Rosa. As soon as she noticed that Rosa was looking her way, she surreptitiously beckoned her over.

Rosa made her way casually in her direction, acting as if she were merely examining the wares on the shelves.

When she stopped beside Valetta, the girl pressed something into her hand. "I have seen Gianni. Not recently but since he came here. He was with certain people. This is a place to start looking. The Resistance," the girl murmured. "If you find him, send him back here for an apprenticeship. My parents will insist I leave to pursue my athletics." Then she moved away and disappeared back into the other room. Rosa opened her hand. A name was scrawled on a torn piece of paper. Aurelio, nickname Lio. That was the only thing written on there. Rosa turned the piece of paper over, but it was blank except for a smudge of clay. It wasn't much to go on. How many men in Karas were named Aurelio? But it was all she had. Tomorrow she would start making enquiries. Hopefully, this Aurelio would learn of her enquiries and come and find her.

Chapter Five

Rosa and Carlotta sat in comfortable chairs at a table in the window of an upmarket teahouse. Rosa was glad that Carlotta had offered to pay for the treat. If she continued to spend at this rate, the coin pouch she had considered substantial would be depleted within a couple of weeks. Carlotta was an exceptional seamstress, and four mornings a week she worked for a lady in Merchant Street. Yesterday had been her day off. Rosa had spent the morning exploring the area around Main Street. It had been interesting but gained her nothing in the way of fulfilling her task. She highly doubted that she would encounter anyone from the Resistance there. The rich might mutter over injustices yet as long as their money continued to flow, they were less likely to want to upset the current order. Some of them would belong, but they would head to meetings somewhere well away from where they lived and worked. Rosa would need to head to the less salubrious parts of the city. She needed guidance as to where to begin.

"Carlotta?"

"Mm?" Carlotta had a mouthful of cake. She had insisted on buying some miniature cakes with their tea. Each was bite sized. They were tasty, yet Rosa couldn't see the point of making them so tiny.

Rosa leaned forward and whispered, "Do you know anything about the Resistance?"

Carlotta stopped chewing and scanned the room, her eyes wide. "I've heard rumours," she whispered back. "Papa doesn't like me to talk about it. He's worried I'll get involved and arrested. It would be damaging for business." She snorted indelicately. She narrowed her eyes at Rosa and picked a piece off the last cake on her plate. "Why?"

Rosa dropped her gaze to her own plate. One cake still sat there. She popped it in her mouth and chewed slowly. Carlotta crumbled her piece of cake and fidgeted.

"I think my brother might have got involved," Rosa replied. "Where could I find them?"

Carlotta sat back in her chair. "How would I know?" Her tone did not match her words and she wouldn't look at Rosa. Rosa hid a smile. Her father might not want her involved, but that wouldn't stop Carlotta being curious and listening to any gossip.

"You must know this city really well. I just thought you might be able to make an intelligent guess as to the best place to start looking for them." Rosa shrugged nonchalantly and waited.

After a moment Carlotta sighed and pushed her plate away. The cake was now just crumbs. "If I were looking for such people, I would begin south of the river. In the backstreets not too far from the docks. Those are places rife with discontent." She shook her head. "But you shouldn't go there. You are as likely to be robbed as to find any information. It could be dangerous. It *is* dangerous. Those parts of the city are full of discontentment. There is high unemployment and crime, and the Assembly does nothing. It is little wonder the Resistance is gaining followers." She sounded wistful, as if she would quite like to join them herself.

Rosa lifted her shoulders and dropped them again. "I have to try, Carlotta. I have to find out what happened to my brother, despite the dangers." She looked around the shop. It was almost empty now, and the other people were paying them no attention.

"The apprentice to Signor Rossi gave me a name. She thought she'd seen my brother with these people. It's not much to go on, but it's all I have."

Carlotta stared at her, then closed her eyes for a moment. "You must tell me before you leave so I will know where you are. If you aren't back after a certain time, I can inform Papa. He will know what to do then."

Rosa opened her mouth to protest. She didn't want them involved, but Carlotta held up her hand.

"If you don't agree to that I will tell Papa what you are planning, and he will put a stop to it entirely." Carlotta lifted her chin and firmed her lips.

Rosa glowered but Carlotta didn't give way. "Fine. It is probably a good plan. I expect my Papa would be less horrified at my setting off alone knowing someone was keeping an eye out for me."

The two girls returned to the house and Rosa dug out her least fashionable dress and a cloak. She strapped her dagger to her waist and left the majority of her coins behind, taking only a few copper coins. Signor Fiscella was busy out at work, Sophia was with some friends, and they both believed that Carlotta was entertaining Rosa. Once she was ready, she said goodbye to Carlotta who stood at the front door biting her lip.

"Good luck!" she said.

"Give me three hours before you tell anyone, please," Rosa implored. Anything less wouldn't give her much time to ask around. She had to get there first.

Carlotta nodded and shut the front door behind her. Rosa took a deep breath and strode away towards the River Tino. The city was laid out in a grid, and she supposed that it would make it easier to find your way around. But it still confused her at the moment. She knew to stay well away from the narrow alleys that seemed to separate blocks of buildings. Who knew what, or who, might lurk down those? Along the way she passed a couple of temples, both small buildings dedicated to minor deities. But both had open squares before them, and a few people milled around. One had a stylised statue of an owl in the centre of the square. A temple to Efra, Goddess of Owls, then. Once the river came into view Rosa walked parallel to it as she headed west. Towards the docks. She kept an eye on the bridges over the river. The further west she travelled, the less ornate the bridges. Finally, she came to one that was entirely plain yet seemed sturdy enough. As she stepped down on the southern bank a whiff of decay from the river mud hit her and she wrinkled her nose. Drifting to her through the air came the sound of distant raised voices, clanks and thuds. Was that the sound of the docks? Rosa hesitated. Which way should she choose? Three roads led away from the bridge, heading southwards. Although Virona lay to the south, Edoardo had taken her around to the East Gate into the city. Now that she knew the poorer area lay to the south, she understood why. With nothing to guide her, Rosa shrugged and took the middle road. Soon she was walking along dirty streets with houses crammed in tight. They had no outdoor areas, just wooden outhouses. Some of them looked like they might fall apart at any moment. She hoped it didn't happen while someone was in them.

The deeper she went, the worse the houses were. She even passed one that had recently been burnt out. The acid reek of soot lingered in the air. Rosa began searching for an inn. Best place for gossip. She had no idea how to achieve this task. She might have to be quite direct. They surely wouldn't consider her an Assembly informant? None of the people she saw scurrying along the streets, or resting, dull-eyed, outside their dwellings, would meet her eyes. Finally, when her feet were sore, and she thought she had been travelling for nearly an hour – which gave her one hour to search if she was to be back before Carlotta informed her father – she spotted an inn sign. It hung crookedly from the wall and was so stained she had no idea of the name. With her blood pounding wildly in her ears, she pushed open the door and was immediately hit by a thick smoke and beer laden fug. The smell was so thick she could taste it. She took shallow breaths until she got used to it and made her way across the sticky floor to the bar. A beady eyed man with a large paunch stared at her in a rather overly familiar way. She ignored it. Though perhaps she could benefit from her looks to gain information. It had worked before. She gave him a friendly smile – though not too friendly. She swallowed in a mouth gone dry. "Me brother said I could find Lio here," she said, laying on some thicker vowels. "Give us a half beer."

The barman looked her up and down again. "You old enough to drink?" he leered at her, half his teeth missing.

"Course I am!" she cried indignantly. She twirled a copper coin between her fingers. He snatched it from her and filled a half-sized mug with foamy beer. He shoved it towards Rosa. She grabbed it before too much slopped over the side. She took a sip. It was too acidic, though drinkable. She took a gulp and wiped the foam off her lip with her sleeve. The barman stopped eyeing her.

"Well, is Lio here?" she asked, injecting as much impatience into her voice as she could.

"What's a girl like you want with 'im?" The barman asked while wiping off another mug.

"That's my business," she said haughtily.

"What's your brother's name then?" he asked.

"Gianni," she said. "He knows Lio real well."

The barman continued drying the mug with deliberate twists of his cloth. He placed the mug back on a shelf and turned it just so. Then he peered back at Rosa and squinted. "You sure you know what you're doing, askin' for 'im?"

Rosa could only nod. Her heartbeat was so loud she was sure the barman would hear it. He pursed his lips and then opened his mouth to answer. The door banged back on its hinges. A young boy stood there panting.

"Dark Patrol!" he cried. "Dark Patrol is coming." The boy darted off again.

At once the barman cursed and half the men in the room leaped to their feet and made a dash for the back of the room. Rosa's mouth fell open and she sat there holding her half-empty beer mug.

"Best get outta here, girl. You don't want to be caught in here by the Dark Patrol." The barman grabbed the beer from her and made a gesture to the front door.

"I have nothing to be scared of," she said defiantly. Though, of course, she did.

"They won't care none about that. You obviously don't belong here. And someone might spill that you was looking for one of the Resistance. Go."

Rosa blinked and then nodded. She hurried for the front door. What was happening? Out in the street people ran, doors slammed, and the pounding hooves drew closer. Six men on horses were riding up the middle of the road. They wore black and grey uniforms and had swords at their waists. Rosa hesitated as they approached, her mind blank. Self-preservation kicked in at last and she turned to run.

"Oi! You there. Girl! Halt at once." They were talking to her. Adrenaline shot through her system, and she ran faster.

Stupid! If she had stopped, she could have explained she was from out of town and got lost. Now, it would be harder to explain. She had to escape. With adrenaline pumping through her, her breath coming in great gasps, she peered back over her shoulder. They were gaining on her. The streets might be narrow, but no one was abroad to impede them. The locals had gone to ground. She was alone. Before she could think about what she was doing, she reached for her magic.

"By Enara! Where'd she go?" one voice shouted in alarm.

"She's a magic-user! We must apprehend her at once!" declared another. "No doors have opened and there aren't any alleys. You get ahead, you get off your horses and search. She was over there. Hurry!"

Rosa crouched against the building, holding her concentration. She wasn't exactly invisible. If anyone knew what to look for and that she was there, they would spot the blurring. Her magic allowed her to bend light and blur her outline. There was also an element of suggestion to the people around to not look in her direction. But that wouldn't work on these men. They had seen her and were determined. If they came too close, they might notice the blurring.

Two horses thundered past, blocking her escape in one direction. One man remained on his horse in the other direction. Three men dismounted and spread out across the street, slowly moving in her direction. They scanned the ground and the walls and waved their arms around them. Rosa's heart pounded. They were bound to spot her. She pushed herself to her feet. Her only hope was to sneak behind the two mounted men approaching from the direction of the inn. They thought she had headed the other way. She edged back the way she had come, keeping an eye on each of the guards in turn, her back almost scraping along the wall. She was past the three walking. Just the two mounted guards left.

Her foot connected with something with a clank. The empty, broken pot rolled away from her feet.

"There!" yelled one of the Dark Patrol. At once the three on foot converged on her position. She started to run. One touched her sleeve, and she couldn't prevent a gasp of panic. The second made a grab and snagged her cloak. Rosa twisted and the cloak fell from her, but she was off balance and when the third made a grab she couldn't avoid his iron grip.

"Got you!" he snarled.

Rosa screamed and thrashed, and the man hit her on the side of the head. Her feet went from under her, her magic faded and so did the world around her.

.

Chapter Six

Rosa startled awake and sat up. Her breath rasped and her heart thudded in her ears. For a moment she couldn't imagine where she might be. Then it came flooding back to her and she pulled her knees up to her chin and sank her head onto them. She had been foolish, stupid. If she hadn't panicked, she wouldn't be here. She had been so sure of herself, so certain she knew what she was doing and could rescue her brother. So sure she wouldn't make a mistake that drew the Dark Patrol's attention.

After the guard hit her, she had briefly lost consciousness. She had woken to the guard dragging her to a horse and slinging her over it like a sack of potatoes. The guard already mounted had levered her up into a sitting position.

"Try anything and I will tie your hands and feet and let you dangle like so much baggage," he had hissed in her ear. "Understand?"

Rosa had nodded vigorously, unable to speak. Ice seemed to have replaced the blood in her veins. She had heard so many stories about what happened to the magic-users that the Dark Patrol took off the street. *Gianni, I'm sorry. I need someone to rescue me. How am I ever going to help you?* Rosa slumped as the gait of the horse bumped her up and down. The guard held onto her tightly and on one occasion used that as an excuse for placing his hand in a far -too familiar place. Rosa felt indignation chase away a little of the ice and she applied her elbow to suggest he move his hand. With a hiss he had dropped it back to her waist. It was still discomforting, though probably better than falling off the horse and breaking her leg. Although if she fell off, she might stand a chance of running away. The journey had lasted for ages. They had ridden through the city and out of the north gate. She had then got her first decent look at the new Assembly Headquarters. The building that had once housed their research facility. Maybe it still did. But now layers of secrecy surrounded the place. There were so many rumours. Something grim had happened twenty-five years ago; everyone agreed on that. Though no one knew what, or anyone who did know wasn't talking.

It was an imposing building. It loomed over her as they approached. It could be glimpsed from most areas of Karas, keeping watch over the city and its people.

Rosa sighed and stared around her, despondent. The bed she sat on was a narrow wooden cot with a straw mattress, minus most of the straw. There was also a thin blanket that was most definitely not washed between prisoners. She hadn't yet become cold enough to even touch it. In the corner was a slop bucket, currently empty. Though she would have to use it soon. She pulled a face at the thought. She had never once paid any thought to prisoners and the total lack of dignity they faced. But now she found herself totally baffled as to why anyone would offend more than once and risk coming back to a place like this. They had even taken her beautiful dagger. For 'your own safety', they had said. Would she ever see it again? Not that it had proved much use to her so far. But her papa had spent many hours making it for her and she wanted it.

The tiny window high in the wall let in a thin trickle of light, but it was impossible to tell how long she had slept. She hadn't meant to sleep at all. She had simply lain down and closed her eyes out of pure boredom and anxiety. How long would she be left alone here? Her stomach rumbled uncomfortably. It must be close to lunchtime. They must feed prisoners on a regular basis, surely? Anxiety was a sharp pain as she considered the fact that she wasn't a normal prisoner. She hadn't attacked anyone or stolen or vandalised anything. She had simply shown the Dark Patrol that she had magic. Such prisoners as her might be left to rot. She swallowed and tucked her suddenly cold hands between her knees. Footsteps along the corridor brought her head up sharply. A loud rap on the door had her heart pounding again.

"On your feet, prisoner and stand against the back wall!" the voice was harsh, and she leaped to obey, her legs quivering.

The locks clanked and groaned, and the door was shoved open, letting in stronger light and making her squint. A man was silhouetted against the light. He stepped into the room carrying a tray. He dumped it onto her cot.

"Food," he said. "I'll be back in one hour to collect the tray and the spoon." He glared at her as if already suspecting her of harbouring designs on the spoon. Then he turned around and left the room.

Rosa ran for the door. "Wait!" she called. But the door slammed shut and the locks clanked. She was alone again. She stepped over to the tray and peered at the contents of the bowl that sat on it. A thin soup or stew with oil floating on the top. There was also a glass of water. The glass was covered in fingerprints. Nausea rose in her stomach, but she fought it down. Rosa determinedly picked up the spoon. She sat down and manoeuvred the tray onto her lap. She closed her eyes and began to eat. It tasted … of nothing really. The stew, or gruel, or whatever they might name it, was mostly water. No one was going to thrive on this fare. She wistfully remembered the wonderful lunch she had eaten at the Fiscella house. Her spoon froze halfway to her mouth. Carlotta would have spoken to Marco by now. Hope rose in her. Surely, such an influential merchant as that would hold sway with the Assembly? He would get her out. She desperately clung to that hope even as doubts swept in. The Dark Patrol had been given a special mandate by the Assembly, to round up the children whose magic was twisting them into something dark. Once she had heard them referred to as Darklings. That couldn't happen to her. She was too old. But it might be that the Dark Patrol and whatever Assembly department they were under, didn't care. Marco had implied that they now took anyone with magic. It was a vendetta. Would they simply deny her existence? Blame the people around that inn for murdering her and disposing of her body? Rosa couldn't finish the last mouthful of her gruel and the spoon clattered into the bowl. She pushed the tray away and leaned back against the wall.

She might be kept in the dark for the rest of her life, never seeing her papa again. Never knowing what had happened to her twin. A tear tickled its way down her cheek.

The guard had returned and removed the tray, sniffing in disdain over the leftover gruel. "You'll regret not eating that later," he said. He picked up the spoon and eyed it before leaving, as if making sure it really was the one he had brought. Then the door was locked again, and she lay down to try and shut out the world. It must have been at least a couple of hours later when there came more footsteps along the corridor. Two sets this time, one softer than the other. Rosa barely paid attention. She doubted it had anything to do with her. But the sound of her stubborn lock had her sitting upright. Again, she was greeted by the silhouette of a man. It was not a guard, and he carried a lantern. Rosa stared at it. The soft light that fell from it was lilac. So, this was the fabled Frith light that was unique to Karas. She had noticed the flatter, oval shaped globes in the area around the Fiscella home but had not paid attention.

"You will wait outside along the corridor," the man said. His voice was calm and had the accent of someone from a lower class than the Fiscellas, though not a rough accent. Someone who worked for a living and was neither rich nor poor.

"She could be dangerous. You know what she is." A rougher voice. Another guard perhaps?

"I think I'll be just fine, thank you." The man's tone brooked no argument. The guard huffed but she heard his footsteps march away.

"Now then, we can talk in peace." The man came forward and set the lantern on the floor. Rosa's gaze was still fixed on it.

"Should've asked for a chair," the man murmured as he realised there was nowhere to sit. "Could you pass me the blanket?" he asked.

Rosa was so bemused that she didn't even consider the state of the blanket as she passed it to him. He folded it, placed it on the floor and sat cross legged on it. "Hmm. Only slightly better than the floor." He looked up then and smiled at her.

Rosa was struck by how young this man was. He was clean shaven and had a mop of thick dark hair. He couldn't be more than a few years her senior. "Who are you?" she asked, her voice no more than a hoarse whisper.

"I am Assembly Man Garthwin," he said. "I am here to interview you."

"Interview? But I thought that those taken by the Dark Patrol…"

"Were hidden away and never seen again?" The man's face screwed up into bitter lines. "I and some of my colleagues are trying to prevent that, signorina?"

"Rosa d'Alessi," she said. She saw no reason to keep her name from him If he knew that she was from out of town and also was known to the Fiscella family, it might help her.

"So, where do you live, Signorina d'Alessi?"

"Virona."

Garthwin's eyebrows twitched upwards. "Well, you are a long way from home. I think you had best explain what you are doing in Karas, and the events leading to your arrest."

Rosa bristled slightly at the term 'arrest'. It had felt more like an abduction. Nonetheless, she proceeded to explain everything to this Garthwin. He had an open and friendly face, and his eyes were bright and warm. It seemed genuine too. Though she could be utterly wrong, and this was some trick to obtain a confession from her.

"Is my brother here too? Do you have Gianni here?" she asked at last.

Garthwin frowned. "I don't know. Does he have magic too?"

Rosa shook her head.

"Hmm. Then he would have been arrested for something else. You say it was about two months ago that he stopped writing?"

Rosa nodded this time.

"Well, there was a rally organised by anti-Assembly people and some of them were definitely from the Resistance. The guard and the Dark Patrol broke it up and then there was a bit of a riot. People were injured and others arrested. I will ask around for you. In the meantime, I will also see what can be done for you."

"I have done nothing wrong!" Rosa declared. "I was simply looking for my brother and then panicked when those great horses came at me. I used magic but I am too old for the magic to twist. Surely they know that?" Her tone had started out defiant yet ended up imploring.

"I know that. But certain factions in the Assembly don't seem to care. They want every magic-user banished from the city Very short-sighted in my opinion, but I am a junior member so only a few listen to me. Still, I do what I can to help." He patted Rosa on the hand. "I will get you out of here, Signorina d'Alessi. Don't you worry. Now, I will go and see if your brother is around here. Even those taken by the Dark Patrol are recorded. Not straight away, but eventually. If your brother was arrested there will be a record of him."

"Has Signor Fiscella come for me at all? Only he will know I am missing by now." She bit at her lip. He would have searched for her, wouldn't he? He must surely be very worried, after losing a second d'Alessi.

"He would not have been allowed up here. I will send him a message to let him know you are well," Garthwin promised. He pulled himself to his feet, took the lantern that had not flickered even once and, with a quick wave to her, left the room. It took just a few seconds for the guard to stomp back and re-lock the door. But now Rosa had hope. She might learn of her brother's whereabouts, and it seemed she would get out of here. She trusted this Garthwin.

Chapter Seven

Rosa chewed at her lip as she waited for Garthwin to return. Her muscles were tense, and every noise had her flinching. She forced herself to lie down and try to sleep. She dozed briefly but footsteps thudding along the passage had her shooting to her feet. They were heavy footsteps. It felt like her heart sank right to her toes. The guard was coming back. He told her to stand at the back while he dumped down another tray with another bowl of slop. Even if it had been the most delicious of foods, she couldn't have eaten it. Her nerves had tightened her throat and made her stomach churn. Plus, there was the smell from the now used bucket. She had pushed it as far from the bed as possible, yet she was aware of it all the time. A reminder of her continuing humiliation.

Was Marco Fiscella even now demanding her release from the Assembly? Who would get her out of here first? Marco Fiscella would come and try and rescue her, wouldn't he? But how would he know she had been arrested? He might be able to make discrete enquiries for her whereabouts in the poor quarters of Karas, but would anyone tell him what had happened? No. If she were to get out of here, it would be by Garthwin's hand.

The tiny slice of sky she could glimpse through the window darkened. Eventually it was so dark she had trouble seeing her own hand waving before her face. She had never known complete darkness before. Even at home in the middle of the night the sky lent some light. But her windows at home were large with gauzy window coverings and shutters that she could choose to leave open.

As the night dragged on Rosa's mind sank into darker thoughts and her hope slowly faded. Garthwin wouldn't be able to convince anyone that she should be released. Her brother had been in that rally, and he had been killed and she would never find his body. She and her father would be left, wondering, forever. She wiped away the moisture from her eyes with her sleeve.

She gritted her teeth. She was Rosa d'Alessi! She didn't cry. She always found a way. Garthwin would come through for her, or she would find a way to use her magic to escape. She scowled and crossed her arms and stared fiercely at the door, daring it not to open.

There were rosy tints of light sneaking through the window before she heard the double set of footsteps again. She sighed and blinked her gritty eyes. She had struggled to sleep and was too weary for the sound to perk her up much. She also didn't want to hope in case he had failed.

The door was pushed open and Garthwin entered with his lantern. He stood in the doorway and held the lantern up. It threw strange shadows across his face. Still she could see that he was smiling.

"Come on then, Signorina d'Alessi."

"Where to?" she asked suspiciously.

Garthwin chuckled. "Outside. You are free to go."

Rosa grinned so widely her cheeks hurt. She rushed to Garthwin and threw her arms around him. "Thank you! Thank you!" She pulled back and smoothed her dress, warmth flooding her cheeks. As she did so she noticed a blue oval pendant peek from around his neck. "Sorry," she murmured.

"I don't mind. Not often pretty girls hug me. Make the most of it, I say." Garthwin cleared his throat and straightened his clothing, the pendant hidden under his shirt once more. He indicated that she precede him along the corridor.

Rosa's feet sped up the further along she walked, desperate to be out in the open once more and know she was free.

"Unless you know where you are going, you'd best wait for me," Garthwin said.

Rosa slowed and took a peek at him. He didn't seem annoyed at her. In fact, his face showed nothing except understanding. The guard, however, was glowering and muttering. But she cared nothing for his opinion on anything.

Rosa stumbled, though she immediately found her balance once more. Her brother! She hadn't asked after Gianni. Guilt stabbed her.

"What about my brother?"

Garthwin's face became regretful, and her heart stuttered. "I have not been able to locate him here. It looks as if he was never arrested. Sorry."

Rosa flattened a hand to her chest, where her heart had begun beating again. "I will have to continue with my enquiries then."

Garthwin took hold of her arm. It was a firm hold, though not tight. His gaze was intense. "You need to leave Karas, Signorina d'Alessi. If you are taken by the Dark Patrol again, I really don't think I'll be able to save you. You have been set free on the condition that you leave the city. Magic-users are not welcome here anymore."

Rosa pulled away. "That's not fair!" she cried. "And I can't leave without news of Gianni. I can't."

"No. It isn't fair." He wiped at his nose with his sleeve. A habit that showed his roots were among the common people of Karas, not the rich. How had he managed to obtain a valuable position in the Assembly?

"You have been given one full day to gather your belongings and arrange to leave the city. After that…" he shrugged.

"Will the Dark Patrol actually come looking for me, specifically?" she asked, alarmed. One day was not enough time!

"I don't know. They are a bit of a law unto themselves. Something else I want dealt with."

Rosa hadn't paid much attention to their route; all the corridors looked the same. When they came to a staircase Garthwin led her upwards, the guard trailing along behind.

Rosa peered over her shoulder at him. "He's here to make sure I leave, is he? Make sure I don't just fancy staying on another few days in your luxury accommodation." She sneered.

The guard muttered but looked away. Garthwin snorted. "He's here to make sure you don't dart off down one of the other corridors and find out all the dark secrets of the Assembly."

The guard glowered at him. Rosa blinked. He had almost sounded serious. Were there dark secrets here? Rosa shook her head. The only secret she wanted to unravel was what had happened to her brother.

Finally, they reached the top of the stairs and headed down more corridors. A guard stared at her severely as Garthwin led her out into the cool morning. Rosa took in a deep lungful of the fresh air. It was just past dawn, with a deep blush of orange on the horizon.

Garthwin clasped his hands and fidgeted. "Er. I'm sorry but they wouldn't agree to any transport. You're gonna have to walk back."

Rosa turned and stared at Garthwin, then the distant city.

"I reckon they did it to use up some of your time. They want you gone, Signorina d'Alessi." Garthwin's voice was soft. "I would do what they say. Make sure you are away before tomorrow morning." He pulled a piece of paper from his pocket. "This is a pass to allow you back through the gate into the city." He held it out and Rosa took it and clenched it tight in her fist. He dug into another pocket and presented her with her dagger, a shy smile on his face. "I thought you'd want this back."

Rosa clutched it to her chest, her eyes prickling in the way that presaged tears. She blinked them away.

"Thank you. For everything."

Garthwin looked down at his shoes and nodded. "Signor Fiscella had been asking all around the city about you. Frantic with worry. I have set his mind to rest, and he awaits your return. Good luck." Garthwin smiled awkwardly and re-entered the building.

Rosa stood forlornly, gazing along the road back to Karas. The guard cleared his throat, and she strode away, tucking the dagger into her cloak.

Chapter Eight

Rosa's feet ached and she was bone weary by the time she found herself once more crossing the river into the south of the city. The guards had taken her pass at the north gate and examined it carefully before telling her to 'move on'. She perhaps should have returned to the Fiscella house to reassure Marco and Carlotta now that she was out of prison. But she found she couldn't face them, not yet. She was angry and humiliated and feared that Marco would prevent her from searching for her brother again. She had to try again to find word of Gianni. If she was going to have to leave by tomorrow morning, she had little time left. She didn't want to return home, her tail between her legs, a failure. Her father would simply nod and arrange for the lawmen to become involved. She would burn with humiliation. Everyone would whisper that he never should have sent a girl, a very *young* girl, to do a man's job. No. She couldn't have that. She straightened her shoulders and began searching for a suitable person.

She wanted a boy or young man who was dressed roughly and appeared to be watching the street. It didn't take long to find a likely lad. He was maybe twelve and was using a small knife to pick at his fingernails. Rosa marched up to him. He blinked at her and then scowled.

"Ere, what you up to?" he asked.

"I am looking for the Resistance," she declared. "My name is Rosa d'Alessi and I was told to find Aurelio, or Lio as he's known. My brother, Gianni, has gone missing and I am looking for him. I'll be in the neighbourhood for a while. Pass it on. Thank you." Rosa marched away and didn't stop until she rounded a corner. She slumped against the wall, trembling and peeped round. The boy tapped the knife against his teeth, shrugged and jogged away. Rosa immediately followed.

She had never tailed anyone before, and it was exhausting. After her night of no sleep, she slowly dropped further and further behind the boy. Something slid under her foot, and she had to catch herself. When she looked up again, the boy had disappeared.

"No!" Rosa thumped the wall with her fist and bent over to catch her breath. For the first time she took note of her surroundings and her heart lurched. She was in a dim and narrow alleyway. The bitter tang of what she imagined must be some kind of illegal drug, mixed with that of litter and other filth she tried hard not to think about. Behind her the alley stretched on into dimness. Ahead was brighter. With misgiving settling deep into her chest, she headed forwards, towards the light.

She came out onto a street piled with litter. Terraced houses lined both sides. Two nearby had boarded up windows and the rest were narrow and cramped, the windows dark and unwelcoming. As she wandered along, a net curtain twitched at one window. Rosa chose to ignore it. A door creaked open behind her, and her heart sped up. She walked faster.

Someone stepped out in front of her, and she squealed.

"Oh now, young lady. No need for that." The voice belonged to a woman. Rosa blinked at her and threw a nervous glance over her shoulder. No one was there. The woman was in rough though clean clothes with an almost white apron over the top. Her hair was pinned up in a bun and she smiled brightly at Rosa. Her cheeks were rosy, and her eyes twinkled.

"You must be exhausted traipsing around these streets. And by the look of you, you don't rightly belong around here, dearie," the woman tutted gently. Then she leaned in conspiratorially. "Now old Maria hears what goes on. I know who you're looking for. I can get a message to 'im."

"You know Aurelio?" Rosa almost wept. At last!

The woman made a shushing motion. "You just come along into my little house, and you can have a drink while we wait. Yes?" The woman laid a hand on Rosa's arm and began to gently guide her towards the house beside them.

"Okay. I could do with taking the weight off my feet for a bit. You'll send word to Aurelio?"

"Now don't you worry none. It will all be okay," the woman said. The door opened as they reached it and a girl of a similar age to Rosa peered out. They bustled Rosa inside, rather more forcefully than seemed necessary. Rosa looked around her as Maria bustled her to the stairs. It was very plain with a desk next to the stairs, a cupboard, shelves stacked with mismatched items, and a couple of chairs that would look more at home in an office. Though someone had placed cushions on them to make them look more comfortable. Rosa's brows twitched.

"Bella, go get our guest a nice drink, there's a dear."

Was there a strange emphasis on the word 'guest'? Rosa's brows drew down further. Maria directed her towards a door at the end of the corridor. Past a number of other doors. The house shouldn't have that many rooms upstairs. This was more the size of three of these houses. Had they been knocked though? But who would do that? Maria opened the door and Rosa saw a plain and comfortable room. The only items in the room were a bed and a chair, a bowl and ewer for washing and a narrow wardrobe.

"Why not sit yourself down and rest? Bella'll be along soon with that drink." Maria smiled at her, her eyes bright.

Bella appeared a moment later carrying a mug. She handed it to Rosa. Bella was wearing a lot of make-up and her dress made her look like a maid for one of the rich houses.

"Drink up, dear, you'll feel so much better."

"What is it?" Rosa eyed the liquid warily. Something wasn't right.

"Fruit juice. So much more refreshing than plain old water," Maria assured her cheerily.

Rosa took a sip. It was fruit juice. Over sweetened, still she took another few mouthfuls. Until she saw the avid expression on Maria's face, and the resigned one on the girl's. Rosa dropped the mug and shot to her feet. There was a deep bruise under the make-up beside Bella's eye. Someone had hit her. Rosa gasped and then swayed.

"What is the meaning of this?" she said. Or tried to. Her words slurred and the room tilted. She blinked, trying to clear her vision. Hands took hold of her and steered her towards the bed.

"You have a nice lie down, while we get you more appropriately dressed. Then your training will begin." The woman's voice had turned harsh and came to Rosa as if from a great distance. Rosa's brain refused to understand the words. Though at some level it knew she needed to leave, to get up and go. Her arms were heavier than some of her papa's blacksmith tools and her legs had stopped working. It was futile trying to resist the hands that pushed her onto the bed. The deft fingers that began working at her dress. She rolled her head from side to side and tried to shout, but what came out was a garbled moan. Her eyes closed and the world shrank to nothing.

$$Chapter\ Nine$$

Rosa blinked bleary eyes. Her head was too heavy, and her mouth full of sawdust. She lay still and examined her surroundings. Soft bed, plain room… She sat up sharply and her head spun. That woman, Maria. She had kidnapped her! Rosa looked down at herself. She was wearing a similar uniform to the girl who had brought her a drink. A drugged drink. Rosa scowled. She remembered fingers at her clothing as she sank into a drug-induced sleep. They had stolen her clothes and dressed her as a maid. Her fingers scrabbled futilely for her dagger. It was gone. She had lost it again. What by all the Goddesses was going on?

On slightly wobbly legs, Rosa stood and walked to the window. She pulled aside the curtains and grabbed at the frame, giving it a sharp tug. It didn't move. She tried again but it barely rattled. The window was nailed shut. Down below was the street where Maria had met her. Met her, deceived her and drugged her. Rosa wandered to the door. She knew it would be locked, yet she tried it anyway, yanking on the doorknob desperately. She pounded her fist on the door.

"Hey! Let me out. You have no right to keep me here! Hey!" she continued to yell until she was hoarse. No one came. Rosa sank to the floor and leaned her head back against the door. Out of one prison and straight into another. A flare of anxiety had her scrambling to the window once more. The sun was high in the sky. It was well into the morning, nearly mid-day. She had lost half a day already. She was supposed to leave Karas in the morning. Rosa's mouth drooped. Somehow, she doubted this woman Maria would care. She had plans for Rosa that didn't involve her leaving any-time soon. Plans Rosa was certain she wasn't going to enjoy.

Rosa wasn't sure how long she stood leaning against the window frame watching the empty street, but finally noises in the corridor caught her attention. Rosa sidled to the doorway. She would be standing behind the door if they entered her room. If she were to use her magic maybe she could sneak out. Rosa reached for it … and it slipped through her fingers. A noise of protest escaped her mouth. That had never happened before. Fear rose up into her throat. She forced it down and concentrated on her body. Her head still felt as if someone had stuffed old linen into it and her limbs didn't seem to belong to her. The drug was still in her system and was cutting her off from her magic. Designed that way, or a side-effect? She needed to find out if these people were aware of her magic without giving herself away. If they didn't know she would find a way to use it later.

A fist rapped on the door. "I know you must be awake by now, dearie. Stay over by the bed or it will go worse for you. Even if you was to get past me, I have my men downstairs to stop you, and all the doors and windows are locked. They'll rough you up if you try anything."

A key turned in the lock and Rosa had seconds to decide what to do. She lurched over to the bed. She was in no state to fight anyone at the moment. She would bide her time. She crossed her arms and lifted her chin in defiance.

Maria entered, the girl walking docilely behind her with a bowl of steaming food. Maria smiled in a satisfied way when she saw Rosa standing by the bed.

"Good girl," she said, as if she were a dog. "Now, Bella's brought you some lovely stew. You eat it up and then we can begin training you for your new job."

"I'm not hungry," Rosa stated.

Maria stomped across the room and slapped Rosa across the cheek before she knew what was happening. Rosa gasped in shock and raised her hand to her cheek.

"You will eat when I tell you to. You will do what I tell you. Or there will be plenty more of that. There are plenty of places I can beat you what can't be seen. Our clients don't care how we train you, just that you go to them and do as you're told."

"Clients?" Rosa asked. She wasn't sure she wanted to know, but she had to ask.

"I happen to train the most obedient maids and servants for the upper classes in the whole of Karas," Maria said smugly, sticking her nose in the air. She probably thought it made her look haughty. "If the client isn't a hundred percent happy, they can send the girl back. Bella knows what happens to those girls, don't you?"

Bella flinched and the little colour she had drained from her face.

"You want to turn me into a *servant*?" Rosa gaped. This woman was mad.

"No, girl. I *will* turn you into a servant. Very well paid it is," she chortled. "Well, for me anyway. If my girls are very, very good, they get a small wage at the end of each month and think themselves lucky." Maria's face hardened. "I run a business and my girls are in high demand. Occasionally I have to resort to creative recruitment." A cold grin spread across her face. "'Course, if you prefer, I can always find some men who will avail themselves of your assets in a different way. Pretty girl like you would be in high demand. They'll be queuing up for ya." Her eyes glinted like flakes of ice.

Rosa swallowed. She knew what Maria meant. Being a servant was better than that.

"Now, eat," Maria demanded.

Rosa stared at the woman, wondering whether to refuse again. Her face still stung. But that wasn't what decided her. If she were to stand any chance of escape, she needed her full strength. Refusing the food would gain her nothing. Rosa accepted the bowl from Bella and began eating. It actually had some flavour and a decent texture, and she finished every drop under Maria's watchful eyes.

Maria nodded sharply and sent Bella away with the empty bowl. "Now, let's begin." She grabbed handfuls of the bedding on Rosa's bed and yanked it off into a pile on the floor. "Make the bed."

Rosa stared at her blankly. "What?"

"Make the bed," Maria said again. "What do you think a serving girl in a posh house is gonna be doing?"

Rosa clenched her teeth and began to make the bed.

"Those corners ain't neat enough. Do it again."

Maria forced her to make the bed four times before she declared it was 'good enough'. Bella returned with some items made from bronze and silver. Maria instructed her in the correct way to polish them. Then she made her dust her whole bedroom. All the while Rosa was aware of the sun reaching its zenith and beginning to sink. She struggled against the despair attempting to sink its claws into her chest. If she escaped, she would have to leave Karas and return empty handed to her father. Then they would have to get the lawmen involved. If Gianni was part of the Resistance that could land him in deep trouble.

A cuff around the head had her ear ringing and her attention sharply back in the present.

"There ain't no time for daydreaming in your job. You'll be working dawn to dusk."

"All so you can have my wages?" Rosa spat the words out, half expecting another slap.

"For my expense of housing you here and training you. I run a business, not a charity." The woman sniffed. "You get an honest job and a roof over your head and food in your belly."

"I'm sure that sounds marvellous to the destitute of Karas, but I have a home and I would have found a job when I was older. Papa would have seen to that."

Maria squinted at her. "What was you doing, wandering about this part of town then?"

"I was looking for someone." Rosa wasn't going to tell this woman too much.

"Well, you found someone." The woman tipped her head back and roared with laughter. She stood up abruptly, the laughter silenced. "You can have an hour break. Then we'll do washing up, carrying trays and settin' tables." Maria examined her head to toe. "I reckon you will do for old Signor Giudice. He pays extra for pretty maids." Maria leered and Rosa swallowed. She could just imagine what might go on there. She would be little more than a slave, with no recourse to the law. He could behave as he wished.

"Yes. Always good to keep in with the Assembly. Especially these days. I never get raided by the Dark Patrol."

Maria was proud of herself. Rosa had always known that there were unpleasant and even evil people in life. Yet to know it as a distant concept was far different to experiencing it. Maria was proud of the fact that she sold girls into something no better than slavery, and that she could use corruption in the Assembly to keep herself safe. Suddenly, Rosa understood why her brother might have joined the Resistance. If the Assembly allowed this sort of person to thrive, then they needed to be brought down.

Maria left her alone with her dark thoughts, promising to return in an hour. Rosa threw herself down on the bed and the sheet beneath her face grew wet as she cried silently. *I should have been more careful. I should have asked for more information from Valetta. I should have gone back to Signor Fiscella's and asked for his help.*

Rosa rolled onto her back and wiped away the last tears. Perhaps she should never have come to Karas in the first place. What made her believe she had any chance of finding her brother? She lived in a small town where everyone knew everyone else. She wasn't equipped to understand the corruption that pervaded a city like Karas. The bustle and commerce and latest fashions all hid the darkness at its centre.

Maria returned after what must have been an hour and continued Rosa's instruction. They left her room to head for the kitchen. Rosa scanned around but there seemed no easy way to escape. She caught Maria smirking at one point and heat rose in her face. Equal parts embarrassment and anger. Maria knew what she was looking for and knew she hadn't found it. Still, the effects of the drug were wearing off and Rosa could touch her magic again. Maria didn't seem to have any knowledge of her magic. Nothing in her behaviour suggested she did. She hugged her secret to her, prepared to bide her time. She did spot her dagger lying discarded on a table near the entrance. Her heart lifted just to see it again and know it was still in the same building as her. When she escaped, that was coming with her.

Maria made her do things over and over, even when Rosa was certain she had done it correctly. If Rosa dared to suggest that she already knew something she was threatened with the raising of Maria's hand.

"You don't know how I need it doing!" Maria would retort.

It was just easier to go along with what Maria told her and switch off. Though she had to appear to pay attention, or she would receive a painful dig in the ribs from Maria's sharp elbow. The kitchen faced west, and Rosa noted the sun sinking with an equal sinking sensation within her chest. Her feet ached and her fingers were stiff.

"Right, that'll do for today. Back to your room, girl." Maria prodded at her and with heavy steps, Rosa climbed back up the stairs to the plain room at the end of the corridor. The lock clicked behind her.

"Someone'll bring you some grub later." Maria's footsteps stomped away.

Rosa slumped onto the bed, despondent. Soon enough a door creaked open downstairs followed by heavy footsteps. The sobs of a young girl rose through the house.

"I didn't mean anything! It weren't my fault!" a girl's voice cried.

The sound of flesh hitting flesh made Rosa flinch. The girl's sobs took on a more desperate note. A man's voice murmured, and Maria spoke, "Take her to the cell."

The heavy footsteps were accompanied by scrapes and thuds. Was someone being dragged? What was the cell? It was obvious the girl was frightened of it. She had done something that Maria perceived as wrong and she would be punished. Rosa hadn't even seen the girl, but her sympathy went out to her anyway.

Later Bella brought her some meat, cheese, bread and water. The bread was slightly stale, though it was edible.

"Your name's Bella, isn't it?" Rosa asked as Bella placed the tray on the edge of the bed. Rosa eyed the open door behind her. But she wasn't quite ready to attempt her escape yet. She wanted to discover more about the timings and layout of the place.

"I can't talk to you. I've been punished already. I daren't think what they'd do to me the next time…" her voice trailed off in a shudder. She wouldn't lift her eyes and was quick to shuffle back to the door and lock it once more. Rosa sighed. She wouldn't receive any help from that direction. She was on her own. Maria herself came to take away the tray and brought her a large ewer of warm water which she poured into the bowl. She lifted the old ewer.

"Now, you have a nice wash and get your beauty sleep. Early start tomorrow." She smiled broadly, but it never reached her eyes. How could Rosa have thought this woman had twinkly eyes and a friendly face? Maria left Rosa alone with darkness settling over the land. Rosa washed her face and flung the apron off onto the floor before lying on the bed. She couldn't possibly sleep, though she was bone weary. But she needed to at least rest.

Chapter Ten

A noise startled Rosa awake and she sat up, heart juddering. She went to the window and looked down into the street. The street was in darkness. Only a faint silvery light from the moon gave any illumination, but something was moving. Figures were running along the street. Men in dark clothing. A glint in the dark showed bared metal. Did these men have weapons? Thieves or worse, no doubt. Rosa clenched her jaw. Were there any decent people in this city? She shook her head. That wasn't fair. Garthwin was decent as were the Fiscella family and Signor Rossi. Valetta had tried to help her too. She had seen both sides of the city in her short time here. She supposed even Virona had a criminal element. There was just less opportunity there and less wealth to attract the thieves.

A crash from directly below had her flinching away from the window. Shouts and yells and the sound of metal on metal echoed up from the ground floor. Those men had broken into the building. Rosa's chest filled with dread. What would they do if they found her? She scanned the room wildly, but there was nowhere to hide. She eased towards the ewer and bowl. The ewer was quite heavy. Maybe if she hit the first person into the room over the head, she could use her magic to flee past the others in the confusion? They surely wouldn't know how many girls to expect? What were they after? Rosa strained to hear over the noise of her heart thundering in her ears. Thuds and yells and scrapes moved around the house below. Then silence fell. It was almost worse than the clashes and thuds of fighting. At least she knew what was happening and where. Footsteps creaked on the stairs.

"Check the rooms that end. I'll do this end." A soft, masculine voice. It didn't sound like a murderous cutthroat. Though what did they sound like anyway? Rosa's breath was coming in panicked gasps, and she took hold of herself with a sneer. *What are you? Some kind of snivelling coward? Get a grip!*

Rosa gripped the ewer tightly and trod softly to stand behind where the door would open. She waited, keeping her breath shallow and quiet as the steps ceased just outside the door. A rattle of keys and then the lock clicked. The door swung open, and a man stepped into the room. He looked around. Before he could look behind him, or turn around to leave, Rosa swung the ewer at his head. It hit with a thud. The man grunted and collapsed in a heap. Rosa stared at him, eyes wide. Was he dead? He moaned and relief swept through her, followed by a surge of adrenaline as the man at the other end of the corridor called out.

"You okay?"

Rosa took a deep breath and drew her magic around her. Then she stepped over the prone man with a wince and slipped out the door. On silent feet she made her way towards the stairs. The other man was approaching fast, and she needed to get to the stairs before him. There wasn't enough room in the corridor to pass him unnoticed. As she took the first step down, the man passed her within a handspan. She closed her eyes briefly before firming her lips and hurrying down the stairs.

Downstairs resembled the aftermath of a tornado. It was turned upside down. There were still cries of pain and anger, but Rosa didn't want to know what was going on. She stepped around ripped cushions and tipped over furniture. The front door swung drunkenly on broken hinges. Her heart leaped and she crept towards it. She peeped through the gap. Three men stood guard outside. Rosa bit at her lip and scanned around her again. She saw a glint of metal under an overturned table. Her dagger! She grabbed it, feeling more secure just by having it in her hands. She had no idea if there was another way in or out. The door creaked as it swung with the breeze. Rosa inched as close to it as she could and took hold of it with her hand. She eased it open just a little wider. One of the guards was in her way. What to do? She glanced down at her dagger. The tip was fine and sharp. In Karas they must have biting insects too. With infinite care she poked the guard in the back of his hand.

"Ow!" he said, lifting his hand. "Something bit me." He stepped away from the door to grumble to his friends and show them the supposed bite.

Slowly Rosa edged past them. The soft slipper shoes that Maria had made her wear as part of the maid outfit made no noise. They were not going to last long, though for now, they were just what she needed.

Rosa crept to the end of the street, heading in the direction that she had first arrived, and then she ran. She ran blindly, with no direction in mind. As she grew winded, she slowed but kept her magic up. She found herself on a normal street corner opposite a temple no larger than a house. It needed repair and a new coat of paint. Still, like all the Karas temples, the front door was unlocked. Inside Rosa dropped her magic with a sigh. Dim moonlight from some narrow windows trickled to the floor and in its meagre light she could see that there was no one within the temple. There were some wooden seats in rows before a wooden altar. Behind this stood a wooden statue, so worn she couldn't tell what the god or goddess represented in the dimness. But she didn't care. Piled up to the side of the altar were blankets. Rosa grabbed three and shuffled to the furthest, dimmest corner of the temple. There she made a nest and curled up. She was desperate for sleep after her ordeal, and she had not used her magic for such an extended period before. It was exhausting. Not long after she wrapped herself in two of the blankets and laid her head on the third as a pillow, she drifted off to sleep.

Rosa woke early, stiff from lying on the cold floor. She threw off the blankets and stretched out her muscles. Her stomach growled. The light easing through the high windows had that just after sunrise quality. The day the Assembly had declared must be her last in Karas. But it couldn't be. She had to find out what had happened to Gianni. This time she would not be following some random stranger, nor trusting anyone. She would ask at the two hospitals first. If he had been injured, he might have ended up there. Then she would use her magic and sneak around listening to the chatter. Someone would let something slip. She forced out of her mind the thought that in a city the size of Karas it could take her weeks. Right now, she had the pressing problem of what to do for food. There were no offerings in this temple. She could sneak into some of the others. People made offerings to the gods and goddesses sometimes. They were as much to help the poor as to appease the gods. Well, at this moment she was poor. She refused to feel guilty about taking enough food to keep her alive. She wouldn't take much.

Rosa hadn't bargained for the amount of energy that using her magic to sneak around would require. She took far more food than she had planned, and each time guilt rose and made the food difficult to swallow. Once everything was sorted, she would find a way to make a donation to each of the temples.

The sun was once more sinking into the afternoon and the only thing Rosa had learned was that her brother had not been take to either of the city's hospitals. She stood in the shadows down an alley beside the temple she had just stolen fruit from. The food was there for hungry souls, though she still couldn't think of it as anything other than stealing. If she had access to that heavy pouch of coins that Papa had given her, it would be different. Footsteps approached and Rosa pushed further into the dank alley.

"No, we can't stop off for a quick one at the inn! Lio's called a meeting, and we need to be there." The voice was irritated.

Lio! That was the nickname for Aurelio. The man that Valetta had suggested to her. Rosa dropped the last bit of apple and quickly drew her magic around her. The two men were striding away down the street. Rosa followed, keeping to the edges and in every shadow she could find. The two paid no mind and indeed, most folk in the street were too busy with their own affairs to notice a faint blur or disturbance of the air.

Rosa's feet hadn't recovered from her search of the hospitals and soon she gained a limp. But she gritted her teeth and kept up with the two young men. This was the only lead she had. She couldn't afford to lose them as she had the boy.

At last, when she was certain that she could go no further and would have to give up because her feet surely were bloodied stumps in her shoes, the two stopped outside a boarded-up building. They scanned the area but didn't see Rosa in the shadows. No one else was around. They headed round the side and one man lifted a loose board on the window. The other man pulled over a discarded box and stood on it to reach the window opening. He wriggled up and under the board. The second man followed seconds later. Rosa hobbled over to the window and listened. Nothing. Carefully she climbed onto the box and pried up the edge of the board. She peered inside. Nothing but smothering darkness and silence. She strained her eyes and ears. Nothing seemed to be moving. With her heart thumping, partly from anxiety and partly from excitement, she slithered under the board. She half fell, half clambered down the other side. She sat for a moment. No one came to check out the noise. She let the magic slip away with relief. It had become easier to hold onto it for long periods, but it still gave her a headache and made her hungry. She hoped her stomach wouldn't suddenly growl and give her away.

The only route led straight ahead. She crept along the narrow corridor where dust swirled in the air, threatening to make her sneeze. A murmur of voices reached her from ahead. A glow of orange lantern light spilled out of a doorway along with voices.

"How are we getting on?" a strong male voice asked.

"Found two more. We'll keep looking. They wanted to go home."

"We need to find them all. What about Mauro?"

"We dealt with 'im. He won't be harming no young'uns no more."

Rosa knit her brow. What were they talking about? This wasn't the talk of rebellion, action and trouble she had expected. She drew her magic around her again, drew her dagger, and slipped through the doorway. She wanted to see the people inside. A group of twelve men and women of a variety of ages sat or stood casually around the room. One or two were rather well dressed. At the front stood a tall man with wavy brown hair. Before she could decide what to do next her nose tickled, and a loud sneeze echoed across the room. She froze in horror.

Everyone in the room spun to face the door, their eyes scanning the space. The tall man's gaze seemed to home in on her. He had detected the disturbance her magic left in the air. She wanted to meet the Resistance. Here they were.

Rosa let the magic drop but raised the dagger before her, trying to look threatening. Mouths opened in the group and there were gasps. Though not from the man at the front. He raised an eyebrow, and his gaze took her in from head to toe.

"Judging by the outfit I would say you were at Signora Maria's house. Which would make you Signorina Rosa d'Alessi, I presume?"

Rosa's mouth fell open.

"I believe you have been looking for me," the man said with an upward lift of his lips. "And you won't be needing the dagger, I assure you." Rosa let it dip slightly, but holding it made her feel brave, so she didn't tuck it away. This man seemed entirely too calm at finding a stranger in the room. It took a moment for his first statement to sink in. Looking for him? Her eyes widened.

"You are Aurelio?"

The man bowed at the waist. "Indeed. At your service." He reached up and rubbed the back of his head with a rueful expression. "Hopefully you won't feel the need to hit me today or stab me." He chuckled as Rosa's face flooded with heat.

"That was you? I am sorry. I had no idea…" her voice trailed off as Aurelio held up his hand.

"No apology necessary. You were very resourceful. I admire that." He smiled and Rosa became aware of the sparkle in his dark eyes, the wave in his brown hair and his lean torso under a thin shirt. She turned her gaze away, and this time she did put away the dagger.

"I probably should have announced myself, and let you know that we were there to rescue you. As well as deal with Maria."

"How did you know that I was there, and why would you deal with Maria?" Rosa was intrigued. It wasn't what she imagined when she thought of the Resistance.

"We have spies all around the city and hear most of what's going on. I learned of a girl desperate to meet me, who needed knowledge of a missing brother. How could I not look for you?" Again, he smiled, and Rosa found herself drawn to this charismatic man.

"I am only sorry it took us so long to catch up to you and to discover the location of Maria's hideout. As for why we would deal with Maria, that is simple. We stand for fairness and freedom. It isn't only the Assembly that needs to change in this city, Signorina d'Alessi."

"Rosa, please," she said, with her best simper. Aurelio blinked rapidly and ran a hand through his hair in response. If she was going to admire his looks, then she would make sure it worked both ways!

"So, it would seem that both the d'Alessis have skills that the Resistance value. Gianni did mention you had certain talents," Aurelio's tone turned teasing and Rosa narrowed her eyes. She had a feeling that Gianni hadn't just meant her magic. Then it registered fully what he had said. Gianni!

"You know where Gianni is? Is he all right? What happened to him?" Rosa's words tumbled out over each other, the relief and hope a heady drug.

"Yes, yes and that will take a while to answer," he replied. "I think it is time for a reunion. Will you come with me, Rosa?"

Rosa nodded eagerly. Aurelio broke up the meeting and sent the others on their way. Not a few of them gave Rosa an intense and curious inspection on their way out.

"Come then." Aurelio led Rosa out of the boarded-up house, and she followed him down the street.

"What will happen to the girls that Maria forced into service?" Rosa asked him after they had turned into a second street.

"We'll try and find them all, and they can choose what they want to do. Some might want to stay on, as long as they get their wages from now on. We have already found some of them."

Rosa bobbed her head. "It is not what I expected when people mentioned a Resistance."

Aurelio smiled wryly. "No. Everyone thinks rebellion and fighting and shouting slogans of 'down with the Assembly'." He chuckled. "We do some of that. But our sole purpose is to make Karas a decent place to live, for everyone. We want our rulers to be free from corruption and for the guard to deal with thieves and thugs, not catch magic-users and imprison them for no reason. Not to kidnap children and make them disappear." He sighed. "We have a long struggle ahead, and I fear it may take my lifetime to achieve that goal. But if we do nothing, things will get worse. Of course, some of our people do just want to thump the enemy and cause trouble. But we manage them well enough."

Rosa didn't speak and they walked on in companionable silence. She had seen the corruption within Karas, the dark pervading its society. This man had the courage to stand up to that and fight for justice and fairness. A man of principle and passion. No wonder Gianni had joined them.

After a few minutes Aurelio looked towards her, his eyes bright. "Gianni has spoken of you often," he said with a smile. Rosa's eyes drifted to his lips, and she quickly pulled her gaze away.

"It was mostly in fondness. But I got the impression that you often got him into trouble." Aurelio's smile became a grin.

Rosa couldn't help but grin back. "It's true. I was always shirking my chores and dragging Gianni away with me. When the fair came to town and Papa was busy, I would drag Gianni there to watch the fire-eater and the knife-thrower. Even though Papa had expressly forbidden us to go without him." Rosa giggled. "I would always get into more trouble than Gianni, Papa knew us well. But it was worth it."

Aurelio glanced at her again. "I am trying to decide if it was bravery or the trouble seeker in you that brought you to Karas after your brother."

"Oh, it was definitely bravery." Rosa said with the most serious expression she could manage.

Aurelio chuckled. "Being able to become invisible must have been useful for getting into, or out of, trouble as well."

Rosa shrugged her shoulders. "I didn't use it much. I felt bad for Gianni as he has no magic. It seemed like cheating too."

"But you have used it here," Aurelio said softly.

"I use it when I must." Rosa glanced sideways at him. There was something in his voice. Something he was contemplating.

"Would you be willing to use it for a good cause?" Aurelio's bright regard captured hers and she couldn't look away.

She wanted to shout *yes; I will use my magic for you*. But she forced herself to blink and look away.

"For the Resistance, you mean?" she said, her voice only a little breathless.

"Of course. You would be very welcome to stay and join us, either way," Aurelio added. His eyes were full of warmth and intensity.

Rosa found she very much wanted to stay. Not just for the Resistance, but to get to know this man better. His gaze did all sorts of things to her insides.

They continued on in silence and after half an hour Rosa was lost and beginning to flag. She had eaten almost nothing and barely slept. Aurelio stopped outside a non-descript house and knocked quietly on the door. It was pulled ajar, and Aurelio whispered to someone behind it. The door opened wide.

"Come in," Aurelio smiled at her.

Rosa found herself disappointed by the inside of the house. Rosa wasn't sure what she had expected from the hideout of a Resistance leader, but it hadn't been an unremarkable and completely ordinary house. She eyed

Aurelio surreptitiously. She assumed he was one of their leaders. She would have to ask Gianni.

"Go right to the top of the second flight of stairs. He is in the loft." Aurelio indicated with his chin the stairs ahead.

Rosa began to run; then she checked and turned back. "Thank you," she said.

Aurelio grinned at her.

Rosa had to stop and take in some deep breaths by the time she reached the top of the second flight of stairs. She couldn't have said what she had passed on the way. One door stood before her and with a trembling hand she reached out and opened it. A man sat on a bed on the far side, bathed in flickering light from a lantern.

"Gianni!" Rosa leaped across the room to be enveloped in a one-armed bear hug as he rose to his feet.

"Mind my arm, pesky one!" her brother cried.

Rosa pulled back to examine her brother. His hair was even more of a mop than usual and flopped over eyes as dark as hers. His lashes rivalled hers for length, Alessia had been jealous of them too. Though Rosa half thought Alessia had a thing for her brother. But now he was in Karas, nothing was going to happen there.

His right arm was tucked in a sling and as he had hugged her, he had seemed unbalanced.

"What have you done to your leg?" she demanded.

Gianni smiled ruefully. "Can't get anything past you, eh? I had a bad cut. But it is almost healed now. It just needs strengthening. Same as my arm."

Rosa pursed her lips and fisted her hands on her hips.

"I promise I'm okay." Gianni looked down at his feet. "I'm sorry I worried you. I never meant to stop writing. But events kind of caught up with me and then it was too dangerous to write." He lifted his arm. "Besides, it's so hard trying to write with the wrong hand."

Silence fell between them. Normally Rosa would have made some joke, except she was too full of what had happened to her. Too full of gratitude that her brother was alive and well. She couldn't bring herself to tell Gianni what she had been through, not yet. He would feel such guilt. But because of what she had been through, she understood that the Resistance was worth being part of. There was so much to say she hardly knew how to begin.

"What will you do now?" she asked.

Gianni sat down on the bed and ran a hand through his unruly curls. "I'm not sure. I can't live off these people forever. They have little enough as it is. I need a job and a reason to stay in Karas." He eyed her warily as he said this, as if expecting her to argue loudly against his desire to remain.

"You could try Signor Rossi again. His current apprentice, Valetta, might have gone by now. She suggested to me that she would leave him for her athletics." Rosa shrugged. "It would be a good job and a good reason to stay on. A good disguise too." She peeped up at him and was gratified to see his mouth fall open in surprise. She reached up and shut it. "You'll invite the flies in," she said.

The surprise on his face morphed to a frown of concern. "What happened to you?"

Rosa sighed and turned away. He knew her too well. He would know that she had come to take him home if he had got into trouble. He would know that she was stubborn and that for her to so thoroughly change her mind, something must have happened.

"Well, let's see. I was arrested by the Dark Patrol, then kidnapped by a woman who sells girls as maids to the rich and the Assembly members. Then I am brought here to discover my brother is alive and well but forgot to write to his poor sister." She turned back to him with a pout.

"I didn't forget to write," he said.

Rosa punched him on his arm but did ensure it was his left arm. "That is all you have to say?"

Gianni rubbed his arm and his expression rearranged itself into one of seriousness. An expression that rarely graced his face. "I'm sorry, Rosa. It sounds like you have been through a great deal. And it's all my fault. If you want me to come back to Virona and apologise to Papa, I will."

Gianni sat there, his head drooping and guilt oozing off him into the room. A pendant peeked from beneath his shirt. Something familiar to Rosa, though she couldn't place it.

Rosa sat beside Gianni and took his left hand in hers. "I chose to come to Karas to look for you. It wasn't your fault that you were injured and couldn't write. I was naïve to think it would be easy to find you here, and I was foolish. That was why I got arrested. The woman, well, she was just evil, and it was bad luck and impatience that brought me into her clutches. I think that the Resistance is a worthy cause, and you should stay. There is darkness at the heart of

Karas and it needs to be cut out. I will go back to Papa and explain. I may even demand to come back so I can join the Resistance. But you must find a way to let us know how you are doing and find a way to allow us to communicate safely," Rosa said, squeezing his hand. Gianni squeezed it back.

"I do have an idea about that. Some of the lads are fast runners and sometimes we use them for sending messages. I thought we could set up a network of them. You pay them a decent enough amount of money for sending a message, and you guarantee that the lads are independent and uncorruptible."

"How can you guarantee that? Surely if someone offers them more money than they earn for an honest message, they'll take it?" Rosa asked.

Gianni shook his head. "No. We'll make sure the wage they receive is good. There will be records of who does what route, spot checks by other boys. Anyone found to break the rules is out. No fee could be high enough to lose the job forever. They would also be banned from any other job that is run by Resistance or Resistance sympathisers. These boys already pride themselves on their honest work. They practically spit every time the Assembly is mentioned! Also, if anyone is discovered trying to interfere with the boys or their messages, no one will run messages for them, ever. I think it could work." Enthusiasm filled Gianni's voice and his face was animated again.

Rosa dipped her head. "You are right. It sounds as if it could work. But they won't run a message all the way to Virona."

Gianni laughed. "True. But they could take it to one of the carts returning to Virona and get it to you that way."

"Okay. I might let you stay here then." Rosa turned towards her brother and hugged him again. "I am so glad you aren't dead," she whispered.

"Me too," he replied. "And it's wonderful to see you again. I missed you." After a minute Gianni pushed her back and grinned. "Are you proud of me for getting into trouble without your help?" His tone was light once more, back to the Gianni she remembered.

"I am indeed. My work is done." They giggled together.

"What happened to you?" Rosa asked, indicating his arm and leg.

Gianni ran a hand through his hair, making some of it stick up. Rosa suppressed her grin at the familiar sight.

"I joined a peaceful rally against the way the Dark Patrol have been taking children and all magic-users, even though their magic is stable. The Dark Patrol didn't take it well and tried to break it up. Forcefully. The protestors fought back, and it got a bit hairy. A child was knocked down by one of them. He rode on a great big horse, and it reared up. I guess I kind of charged in and pushed the boy out the way. Wasn't so lucky myself. The Resistance got me out of there and patched me up."

"Gianni, Resistance Hero!" Rosa declared, and she was only half teasing. Pride flooded through her for her brother, and she grinned. "I guess we have both had some adventures in Karas." Rosa's eyes were drawn back to the pendant that hung around his neck. She snagged it with her fingers and pulled it out to look at. It was an oval stone or crystal twice the size of her thumbnail. It had a picture etched into its shiny surface. A bird in flight.

"It is a symbol for freedom," Gianni said. "All those in the Resistance have taken to wearing them so we can identify each other."

"Isn't that a bit risky? Won't it make it easier for the Assembly to find you all as well?" Rosa frowned as she let it drop. Her eyes widened. "I know where I have seen one of these before! Garthwin had one!"

"Garthwin of the Assembly? You met him?" Gianni asked.

"Yes. He was the one that got me out of prison. Are you saying that he is a member of the Resistance too?"

Gianni grinned. "He is one of the founding members. These pendants are only dangerous if the guards work out what they mean. Besides, it isn't a crime to belong to a group against the Assembly. Not yet anyway. It is only some of the activities we engage in that might be seen that way. Though that might change with the way things are heading." He shrugged. "We'll keep them for now."

Rosa nodded. "I should probably go and make my own apologies to Signor Fiscella and Carlotta. They might still be worried about me."

Gianni snorted. "Might be? They'll be frantic and scared stiff that Papa will come up here with his beefy arms and give them what they deserve for losing both his children."

"Oh Goddess, he might just do that too! Then I have to leave Karas. It was part of the deal for getting me out of prison. Though I should have already left." Rosa shrugged and grinned mischievously. "They said I had to leave. No one said I couldn't come back."

Gianni shook his head. "Oh, poor Karas, look what you have done. Now you'll never be rid of her."

Rosa dug him in the ribs with her elbow. "So, what can you tell me about Aurelio?" she asked as casually as she could.

Gianni narrowed his eyes. "I am certain Papa has bigger plans for you than a Resistance leader in faraway Karas."

Rosa gave him a sly grin. "Then we won't tell him, will we?"

Gianni burst into laughter. "Oh, you are still the same Rosa. Welcome to Karas, sister."

Rosa smiled back. All was well with the world now the d'Alessi twins were back together.

***

Thank you for reading **The Darkness Within Karas** I hope you enjoyed reading about Rosa and her time in Karas.

To continue the magic and adventure of Karas and beyond jump into **The Shard,** book 1 of The Darkling Duology.

Maybe you can spot a familiar character!

It can be purchased here
https://books2read.com/TheShard

Ancient magic and dark secrets await.

Read on for a sample.

Please consider leaving a review to help others decide whether to buy this book.

***

To claim your **Free** and Exclusive eBook **Origin of The Fallen** use this link and sign up to my newsletter
https://www.janeshandauthor.com/contact

***

The Shard

Book 1 The Darkling Duology

https://books2read.com/TheShard

Chapter One

Nalani clung at the top of the coconut tree, the bark rough against her strong legs. She reached for a coconut and a sensation grazed the edges of her mind. A soft itch that crept into the back of her thoughts. She paused, listening, feeling. She chose to ignore it and carried on collecting the coconuts.

The trees grew on her mother's land and she didn't need to collect them herself; there were employees to do that. But Nalani enjoyed the exercise and felt you should never expect someone to do things you weren't prepared to do yourself. Besides, a wise landowner kept an eye on the land and her mother hardly ever inspected it these days. After she had filled three baskets, she took them to the central collection point. Ikaika, her mother's Head Worker, checked over rows and rows of baskets stuffed with large, juicy coconuts.

"You off now, Miss?" Ikaika asked.

Nalani stretched her arms and grinned. "Yes, I know you don't need my help."

"We appreciate you pitching in, Miss. If it slowed us down, we'd not be so appreciative."

Nalani laughed. "Make sure you tell me if I ever start getting in the way. Have a good evening."

"Good evening, Miss."

The horizon showed the first hints of peach and flame. The beach was peaceful, with only the gentle murmur of the lapping waves to accompany Nalani who spun, dipped and lashed out with one foot. The other foot planted solidly against the soft sand, gritty against her bare skin. Keeping balance on the shifting sand was a skill she had learned over time. She returned to an upright position and stabbed the air like a striking snake, her long knife glinting. She followed this with a slash left and then right. Her skin glistened with sweat. Nalani had worked out for over half an hour and her pulse sped. Her breath came fast. She slowed her movements until finally she stilled and sheathed her knife, placed her palms together before her and dropped her chin. After a moment she raised her head. A haze on the darkening northern horizon marked the mainland. What was it like so far from home?

The next day she found her gaze returning over and over to the north – the mainland, no matter where she found herself on the island. She knew people on the other islands; however, life was much the same there. She had heard stories of the mainland. They had huge cities built of stone or bricks. So large you couldn't make it all the way around in a day. Nothing resembling her own village, small and made of wood and palm fronds. Nalani wandered the edge of the village where a ruby-red orchid caught her attention. A subtle, spicy aroma floated up to her nose. Did the mainlanders have flowers to rival these? Did the mainlanders even have coconuts? Were they as large and creamy as her mother's? They would probably have to import them, and her islands didn't sell to the mainland.

She stared at her own island, taking in every detail, imprinting it on her memory. Lush forests cloaked the dormant volcano at the centre of Naia, vibrant against the azure ocean. Within the forests hundreds of brightly coloured birds chattered; flowers bloomed in every colour. It could not be like this on the mainland, could it? Although they might have something that Naia didn't.

Nalani roamed the island for a couple of hours. Sometimes she ran until her legs ached and her breath came fast. Sometimes she stopped and examined the bright splash of colour from a bird or flower, listened to the clear birdsong above or the rustle of small creatures down in the undergrowth. At last she stopped and allowed herself to think about her actions. Was she saying goodbye to her home? A sharp pang stabbed beneath her breastbone, though whether excitement or anxiety she wasn't sure.

She returned home and took the account books with her to her room at the back of the house. Her mother's house – one day destined to be her house – was a little larger than most. The house stood one storey tall. Three bedrooms, a kitchen and a large living room at the front. Apart from being larger it resembled the other houses of the village. It was made of wood and thatched with palm fronds; large window openings in each room to let the air through with shutters that could be closed and latched at night. Silence greeted her, which meant that Aunt Ellara wasn't here. Her mother might be, but she made so little noise – creeping about insubstantial as a ghost – that Nalani wouldn't know. Five years ago, her mother had asked her to familiarise herself with all aspects of the family business in readiness for the day she would take over. This included the bookkeeping. Nalani had found arithmetic easy at school which meant the accounts were not a problem. Usually. Today the figures seemed to wriggle on the page. After fruitlessly scanning the same page three times she slammed the heavy book shut. She would go and find Aunt Ellara and maybe her mother. She pushed her chair back and made a cursory search of the house. She was alone. Perhaps they were both at the silk cocoonery. Aunt Ellara oversaw silk production on the island and the cocoonery sat on her mother's land. Aunt Ellara had mentioned expanding production. Although it was an intensive process, the rewards were worth it. For some reason, the silkworms of their island produced the best silk thread and the other islanders paid well for it.

Since it belonged to the family business, Nalani had every right to go and visit the cocoonery. It would also get her moving and out of the house. She couldn't bear to sit still today. In her mind's eye she constantly saw the haze of the mainland across the ocean. She wandered through the village and people waved and said hello. She returned the waves and said hello back. She had known these people since she was tiny. Many had taught her when she was a child, or she had played with their children. Now she felt removed from them, with a wall up and withdrawn behind it. Hard now to trust anyone or allow them access to the real Nalani.

A young girl ran laughing down the street, her long dark hair in a tangle. Nalani turned to watch; that would have been her at the same age. She also reminded her of Talin… But Talin lived on Ivaii. Nalani had visited two years ago. Her magic had prodded her to take the journey. Her mother had been bewildered.

"You want to visit Ivaii? Why?"

Nalani had shrugged, not able to meet her eyes. "Why not? We trade with them, don't we?" She had long ago learned that her mother became uncomfortable with talk of her magic, her Gift from Ailana. Nalani often wondered if their Goddess knew what she was doing when she bestowed her Gifts. Surely, she had made a mistake with her?

When she arrived on Ivaii she strode to a tiny house on the village outskirts. Within stood a locked door. Crying and strange harsh growls emanated from within. A woman stood at the door wringing her hands, her eyes wide and rimmed with red in a face devoid of colour.

"You must let me in," Nalani said.

The woman shook her head wildly.

"You must!" Nalani's mind flared. She had to get in there.

"It isn't safe. It will hurt you," the woman whispered.

"Talin, she doesn't know what she is doing. It isn't her fault—"

"I know. I can help her. I promise I can help."

Talin's mother unlocked the door, her desperation obvious in her first fumbling attempt. She dragged it wide enough for Nalani to slip through. The lock clicked sharply behind her. Hot stale air greeted her inside and little light filtered through the shutters, nailed shut. The growling had ceased.

"Talin?" The room resembled somewhere a cyclone had torn through. Shredded paper, pieces of wood, and stuffing from toy animals were strewn around. In the far corner lurked a hunched shape on a stained and ripped mattress. The shape weaved from side to side. The eerie growl sounded again.

"Hello? Talin?"

The shape stirred again, and another sound reached her. It could have been a guttural 'no', but she wasn't sure. Nalani took a step closer and the thing leaped. Nalani reacted instinctively, perhaps guided by her Gift, and grabbed the creature's arms. Her Gift began to draw the darkness from the child and into her. An uncomfortable and tiring process, although one that didn't seem to harm her.

Nalani had deeply buried the memory of the creature's appearance. She only allowed herself to recall the vague impression of wrongness to the sharp bones and a fluidity to the features and glinting eyes and teeth.

After twenty minutes she knocked on the door. "All is well. You can let us out now." No sounds filtered through the door and she began to doubt the mother's courage to do so. Then the lock clicked and slowly the door opened. Talin flew into her mother's arms. There were wails and tears and joy. Nalani watched the family's joy from without, not wanting to intrude. The Gift lay quiescent within her, the task complete. This was not the first time and she knew it would not be the last. She never grew accustomed to seeing such children. Darklings, they were called.

Talin's mother had sent her a letter a couple of weeks later. Talin had returned to school and her friends had accepted her back into their midst. The adults were taking longer. Talin's Gift was Weather Sense. A useful Gift on an island where half the population were fisherfolk.

Nalani shook off her memories and soon reached the cocoonery. The low building, thatched with palm fronds in the tradition of all Naia buildings, squatted in the greenery, a large expanse of mulberry trees beyond it. The dim interior had a distinct, acrid tang, despite the thirty or forty ventilation holes in the walls. The fat white silkworms wriggled on wide trays scattered with the bright green of mulberry leaves, picked fresh each day. Clusters of ovate cocoons nestled on piles of mulberry twigs, ready for collection. The spinning happened elsewhere. The trays were cleaned regularly, feeding happened twice a day and cocoons were checked to ensure they were collected before the moth emerged. Once it did it broke the single thread that formed the cocoon. Some were allowed to hatch in order for them to have an endless supply of eggs.

Aunt Ellara and her mother were deep in conversation with one of the silk farmers at the far end of the building. They didn't hear Nalani enter and she hurried away. Finding them was an excuse to get out of the house. Now she had found them she had nothing to say.

Nalani could hardly sit still or sleep and even her active and fit body struggled with exhaustion. There would be a reckoning soon; she recognised the symptoms. Her Gift's unpleasant way of working up to another mission. This time was different though, far more intense. Her family were going to suffer a big disruption, and no one was going to be happy.

Two days later Nalani sprawled under a coconut palm and stared out at the azure sea.

"Do you really have to go away?"

Nalani turned to Arifi, next to her. Nalani avoided her eyes. "Yes. I have to go."

"But you don't know where exactly, or for how long?"

"No."

"That's just crazy, Nal!" Arifi pounded a fist on the grass beside her. "How long have we known each other?"

"Forever!" Nalani half-laughed then stopped when Arifi grabbed her hand and her for-once-serious expression snared her.

"Exactly. And I still don't understand your Gift."

"Curse," Nalani muttered. As usual her chest felt tight and she couldn't look at Arifi. They had been friends since they were tiny. They had learned to fish and swim together. They had hidden in the jungle to escape their chores. They had climbed the tallest trees and commiserated with each other over injuries and childhood losses. As they grew older, they had talked of boys. But only Arifi had talked of crushes and boys she liked. Nalani was not going to allow any boy close enough to disappoint and betray her. They also never discussed Nalani's Gift. That was off-limits. Nalani tried to pretend it didn't exist, though it hung between her and everyone else like a veil.

"Maybe I could come with you!" Arifi said. She jumped up and began striding about. "It would be an adventure. I've never been to the mainland. It is somewhere on the mainland you're going?"

Nalani nodded and kept silent for a moment. Then she shook her head. "I can't drag you with me, Arifi. Your parents would never let you go anyway. I have no idea where I'm going, or how long I'll be. It's too dangerous. I'll be okay – you know how I can look after myself. One of the best warriors on the island." All true, yet to her shame it wasn't the only reason. She might hate that her power manoeuvred her around like a puppet, however this time it was sending her far away. Perhaps somewhere she could at last feel herself. Somewhere she could fit in. Away from her past.

"You've wanted to leave for a while, haven't you?"

Nalani sighed. She couldn't hide much from Arifi. "Yes, I suppose so." She dug her hand through the warm sand and let it trickle out slowly. "I love Naia." She made an expansive gesture as if to encircle the whole island. "Who could not love this place?"

Arifi studied the area too and grinned. Then she became serious once more. "But…"

"You know how I have been. Nothing has been right since my father … left. Now I find myself being pulled away and I am not entirely unhappy about it." Nalani stared down at the sand.

"Yes, I know how you have been. I'm not certain what you need is out there. However, I hope on the way back to us you find what you're searching for," Arifi said quietly.

Nalani reached up and took hold of Arifi's hand. She probably should have hugged her, but she couldn't do that.

The late afternoon light slanted through the window and puddled on the floor. Nalani curled in one of the squashy chairs in her mother's living room. She had spread the latest account book on her lap. Finally, she had managed to concentrate on the figures; it added up nicely. By island standards they were a well-off family. Generations ago someone had chosen the right land for their enterprises and family members since had cared for those enterprises.

Some slight change in the atmosphere made Nalani turn her head. Her mother stood in the doorway, her right hand clutching her left elbow. Her mahogany curls had fallen across her face. The one trait she shared with her mother. Nalani's hand itched to smooth them back.

"How do they look?" Her mother jerked her head to indicate the accounts.

"Good. Very good," Nalani said, as her mother slid into the room. Her mother wandered aimlessly round the room, trailing a hand over the backs of chairs, lightly touching objects on shelves. She lingered over a wooden boat. Nalani's father had carved it years ago.

Nalani's shoulders started to tense and she forced them to relax. Why was it always this way? She needed to speak to her mother, tell her… "I may have to go away," she blurted.

Her mother briefly glanced at her before her gaze skittered away. Nalani tried to ignore the melancholy that always lurked behind her eyes.

"Go? Where? To one of the other islands?" her mother asked.

"I'm not sure. Maybe further than that," Nalani replied.

"Further?" her mother's voice was hushed, and she had stilled, her hand frozen in mid-air.

Nalani stood and paced to the window. She leaned against the wall. Outside the sky turned purple as the evening drew in. Her mother stood two feet behind her, yet it might as well have been another room. Nalani wrapped her arms about herself. "I think I may have to go to the mainland."

There came a slight rustle and an indrawn breath from her mother. "But you are beginning to take over the business. You can't walk away from that." Her mother's voice had gone flat.

"It won't be forever. There will be a task I have to do and then I will come back."

Her mother remained silent. Nalani turned to her. Her mother's hands were clenched tight enough to make the skin white and her head hung low.

"I will come back," Nalani repeated softly.

Her mother nodded once and shuffled from the room. A room that suddenly felt cold. Nalani slapped her leg and spun round. The wood boat drew her attention, and she ran her hands over it the way her mother had. Her father had shown it to her one day and told her he had carved it. He had tried to teach her to carve wood. They had laughed over her attempts. Had she been too young? She had never tried again. A few days later she and her father had taken a stroll through the village and Kalea, a girl a couple of years older than her, had run past.

"What's her Gift, Daddy?"

Her father had observed her quizzically. "What makes you think she has a Gift?"

"I can feel it."

Her father had smiled. "Looks like you might have a Gift of your own."

He seemed pleased, had smiled broadly. Then the pains had started behind her eyes, and the spasms that left her weak and listless. She grew restless and tore around the village. She went into the forest and screamed. She begged her mother to tell her what was happening, but she didn't know. She overheard whispered arguments between her parents, except she couldn't hear the words or maybe she couldn't remember them. Those days had been dark, but Arifi had been there through it all. She would come and tell Nalani about the mischief she had got up to. She would read quietly to her or just replace the cold compress on her feverish head. She had felt so close to Arifi then and had thought there was nothing she would not share with her.

Nalani clenched her hand and gasped as the mast of the little boat dug into her palm. She sucked at the sore patch. Her father had left in the midst of it all in a boat headed for the mainland. Her mother cried for days and occasionally held Nalani's hand. Though part of her mother was somewhere else, deep in memories of her father and happier days. In her confusion and pain, Nalani had begun putting up emotional barriers. Arifi had ended up on the outside. But she had stayed stubbornly at Nalani's side. Arifi didn't seem to resent the sudden change in their friendship, accepting whatever Nalani was willing to give.

Thirteen years later and her father still had not returned. Your fault, her mind whispered at her. Your Curse drove him away.

Nalani knew her time on the island was nearly done. She had one more goodbye she needed to make. Koa had been her friend for only a year less than Arifi. At school the three of them had been inseparable. He had returned yesterday from a long fishing trip and she couldn't delay this any longer.

Nalani found Koa squatting on the soft sand mending a net. Her shadow fell across him and he peered up. He began to stand, and she waved him back down and knelt beside him. His smile was wide and hopeful, as always when she approached him. One of the reasons she avoided him these days; she hated to hurt him all over again. When would he stop hoping?

"I wanted you to hear it from me, rather than the gossips," she began.

His smile faltered and his brows drew together.

"I am leaving Naia for the mainland." Nothing like getting straight to the point!

Koa's eyes widened and his hands stilled. Emotions chased across his face. "What?" he asked.

"I have to leave. Soon." The salty breeze off the ocean lifted her hair. The dark haze on the horizon pulled at her attention.

"But you can't!" he said. "What about your family? Arifi…" He paused. "Me."

Nalani closed her eyes with a deep sigh. "I have told them."

"You told them before me?" The furrow between Koa's brows deepened.

Irritation spiked through her and she stamped it down, digging her hands deep into the warm sand. "Why would I tell you before my family? And Arifi has been my friend for longer than you." Koa flinched. "We are friends, Koa, which is why I felt I owed it to you to tell you in person."

Koa glared at her for a moment then nodded, his dark expression replaced by a wistful one. "They say absence makes the heart grow fonder," he murmured.

"You need to find someone else," Nalani said gently. "I am not right for you. I told you that last year. You need to find a nice girl, like Arifi."

"Arifi!" Koa laughed briefly. "When will you be back?" he asked, changing tack.

Nalani turned her head away. "I don't know. I don't even know yet where I am going. Just that it seems to be on the mainland." She stood up and Koa jumped up too. "Goodbye, Koa," she said.

He stepped closer, a hand outstretched and she stepped back. He let his hand drop back to his side. "Goodbye," he said.

Nalani spun on her heels and strode away from him. It had been much easier when she hadn't known he felt more for her than friendship. She was sure she had never given him any sign; not intentionally. She tried to be kind last year when he asked to court her, but he became heated and suggested she turned him down because of his lower rank. As if! When had she ever cared about any of that old-fashioned nonsense? Maybe after she left, he would move on and find someone else.

"Mother, I have to go. Why can't you understand?"

Her mother's dark eyes were filled with the usual confusion and pain, then she turned her face away. "It's just like it was with your father. You're just like your father," her mother whispered.

Nalani drew back. A little shard of ice wormed into her heart. "Don't talk about him."

Nalani grabbed the bundle of clothes from her bed and shoved it into her pack. Aunt Ellara pottered in the kitchen, gathering some supplies. Tactfully staying out of the way while mother and daughter had this conversation. Again. The first three times Nalani had been polite and patient, and all the time the itch grew into an unbearable fire. Now it was painful and dominated her thoughts to the extent she could scarcely string thoughts together. Certainly, her patience was at an end.

The beautiful conch shell she had found when she was a little girl rested on the top of her bookcase. Without thinking too hard about it, she grabbed that too and pushed it in amongst the clothes. She strode to the kitchen. Her mother silently followed. Nalani could feel the misery rolling off her. The ice melted away and she desperately wished she had words for her. However, too much lay unsaid between them already. Nalani didn't know how to bridge the gap.

Aunt Ellara's familiar plump figure bustled about in the kitchen while she murmured to herself. Her deep brown hair was now sprinkled with grey, clasped up in a bun by palm fibres. Her sarong and shirt were covered with intricately embroidered sea horses – her favourite sea creatures, bright blue against a cream background. Nalani's mouth quirked and her eyes prickled. She loved her. Yet despite that there existed that careful space, that wall between her and Aunt Ellara. The same wall that held everyone out. But would she have let Ellara in if she hadn't been the sister of her father? At least she didn't have his green eyes.

Aunt Ellara turned around and her mouth curled up into a broad smile. Her gaze flicked behind Nalani and the expression faltered. Her eyes filled with compassion. She opened her arms wide to Nalani. "Honey, I am gonna miss you something terrible."

Nalani awkwardly moved forward into Aunt Ellara's warm embrace. A place she had not been for years. "I will miss you too," Nalani said, her voice quavering. The burning in her mind faded back. Did the Gift know that at last she was moving towards its goal?

She became aware of the presence of her mother behind her and an ache filled her chest. It should be her mother hugging her goodbye. But they had not touched for years. They could barely find enough common ground to hold a conversation.

When Nalani pulled free of Aunt Ellara's embrace she risked a glance at her face. Aunt Ellara's eyebrow lifted.

"What?" she muttered, and Aunt Ellara jerked her chin, to point over Nalani's right shoulder. Nalani stiffened and turned her head.

"Nalani," Aunt Ellara whispered.

Nalani hesitantly raised her head again. Aunt Ellara raised both eyebrows this time and Nalani sighed. She turned around. Her mother stood in the kitchen doorway, her face wet with tears and her arms hanging loose at her sides. Nalani moved towards her mother, the effort akin to wading through the ocean swell. She opened her mouth to speak and her mother shook her head.

"No. I know you have to go. I don't understand any of it. Still I know I can't stop you. Come and give me a hug goodbye."

Nalani's eyes widened, then she stepped up to her and was tugged into her slender arms. Her mother had so little spare flesh. When had she become that skinny? The faint spicy aroma of orchid enveloped her and transported her back to when she was a small child, and her mother would hug away her troubles. Her own arms tightened around her mother's thin shoulders before she gently pulled away.

"I'm sorry," she said, though she couldn't have said which of the many things she was sorry about.

"Good luck out there, my daughter. Keep in touch. Let us know when you arrive wherever it is you are going."

Nalani nodded and her mother trudged away.

Aunt Ellara and Arifi accompanied her to the beach, helping to carry the large woven basket. Her aunt hoped the local silk within could be sold and give her enough money to live off at her destination. Nalani drifted along and took in all the sights of home – the cosy palm-thatched houses, the stands of palm along the beach and the vibrant green of the dormant volcano rising behind her village. They approached the beach and the briny scent of fish and shellfish reached her from where the fishing boats rested. A smell she knew would always remind her of home, along with coconut.

The little boat that was the first part of her journey bobbed on the waves at the end of the pier. They stopped and Arifi hugged her hard. Nalani gave her a stiff hug in return. Arifi seemed not to notice.

"Who am I going to fish with and swim with and mess around with now?" Arifi said, pounding Nalani's shoulder.

"Ow! Are you trying to break me?"

"Would serve you right for deserting me," Arifi replied, her big eyes mournful.

"I'm sorry," Nalani said. Sorry she was leaving her, but not sorry too. Stomach churning with the unknown yet also filled with anticipation. So many conflicting emotions she didn't know what to feel.

Nalani wished to mark Arifi indelibly on her mind, like she had with Aunt Ellara, not knowing how long it would be before she saw her again. Not that she could ever forget anything about her: Arifi was her best friend. Still she stared at her. She stood as tall as Nalani. Her hair a shade lighter than black and cinnamon coloured eyes. She was slim, though not in the bony way of her own mother now. She had shape to her, and her face drew much attention. A dozen of the local boys mooned over her. Nalani wished that Koa was one of them. Their parting yesterday had been awkward.

Aunt Ellara pushed a small package into her hands. "For the first part of the journey across to the mainland, honey. A taste of home," she said, before giving her one last hug. "I know you gonna be okay. You always had to know how to do everything, learn every skill that existed. Never settling to one thing. I think you can adapt to anywhere and I know you'll be careful. I hope you get everything settled and come back to us." Aunt Ellara held her gaze for a moment.

Could she be referring to more than the mission her Gift was sending her on? Aunt Ellara had always understood her better than anyone. Accepted all her faults without complaint or hurt. Nalani bent her head and sniffed the package. Her aunt's special coconut cake. She closed her eyes for a moment at the rich aroma, then waved and gathered up her bags. The boatman helped her into his swaying craft and cast off. He would take her to a larger ship that could cope with the deeper ocean. She faced a three-day journey to the mainland. Then who knew how long her journey would be? She watched her life recede to the sound of splashing oars and the Gift gave a happy buzz in the back of her mind.

Chapter Two

Nalani hurried along the lane which led her unerringly to Merchant Street, trying hard to ignore the stares, fighting the impulse to curl her shoulders and throw the end of her cloak over her hair. Her long linen dress, so alike those around her, only seemed to accentuate her differences, her height, her hair, her complexion just those few significant shades darker than theirs. The scrutiny made the skin between her shoulder blades tingle. Some stares were openly admiring, as if she were an exotic bloom. Others were directed from beneath frowns, a slight tightening to the lips. Those left a hollow beneath her ribs. She was overly conscious of her statuesque figure; the simple lines of her dress did little to hide her curves, of which she was usually proud. For once, she would welcome the slenderer figure of Arifi.

The large woven basket carrying her precious goods bumped her thigh as she slowed at the end of the lane, before taking one step out into the street. She stopped for a moment – she always did – in wonder. There was nothing like this at home.

Merchant Street was vibrant with a clash of colours, scents and sounds. The fresh scent of lemons mingled with the sweetness of pastries and was joined by the sharp richness of herbs, sausages and vegetables. The voices of caged chickens squawked in concert with those of the numerous vendors encouraging potential customers. Three small children dodged laughing between a vegetable seller's trestle table and the neighbouring one upon which baskets of deep-purple figs were positioned. A ball pattered out and along the paved street, the children in noisy pursuit. Their little knees pumped up and down at the hem of their pale tunics.

Nalani inserted herself into the bustle, narrowly avoiding a collision with the boisterous children, and started strolling along the street. Lining the street on both sides were respectable shops and cafés; their owners had no need to shout for customers. Women with baskets milled in and out of the shops, most in pairs or groups, some with servants to carry the baskets, the servants one step behind and scurrying to keep up. The far end of Merchant Street opened out into a square in front of a public bathhouse. Men in short-sleeved tunics over loose trousers stood to the left, and to the right were women in high-waisted dresses, simple sandals peeking from below the hems. Colourful as a flower garden, they gossiped while they waited to enter and be bathed and pampered. The street gleamed in the sunlight, cream walls below bright red roofs. Above them the central Temple of Enara watched over the city with benevolence. The gentle curve of its azure dome graced the skyline. Perched comfortably atop the dome was a cupola, its bell silently waiting for Fifth Day, so it could ring out across the city calling the citizens to worship.

Nalani was tempted by the tantalising hint of cinnamon and vanilla sweetness from the pastry shop, but she was here for business.

She headed for a shop halfway along the street. A tiny alley lay to the side and after ensuring no one was paying her any attention, she slipped down it. She rapped on the side-door which was yanked open almost at once. Faran stood in the doorway as if he had been waiting for her.

"Nalani, so wonderful to see you. As always you rival the Priestesses of Enara themselves—"

"Just let me in," she interrupted.

The man grinned and bowed theatrically, unperturbed by her abruptness. "Your wish is my command." With an agile twirl he moved into the workroom that lay behind his fabric shop and made room for her to enter. The bright lavender-pink glow of his Frith lights gleamed in the thick curls of his dark hair and made his dark eyes glitter. Once his manner had seemed offensive and had made her anxious. However, now she knew he meant nothing by it. It was all part of being a merchant. The sales patter ended up infiltrating their whole lives.

"What have you brought me today?" he enquired, cheerful as ever.

"You told me you were low on blue and red and I thought we could introduce two new colours." Nalani removed the wrapped bundle from her basket, placed it on a table and gently unwrapped it to reveal layers of the finest silk. Faran stepped forward and stroked the glimmering fabric almost reverently. The brilliant azure and fiery red of the top layers were Faran's best sellers. Beneath these were her two surprises. Carefully, lest the slippery material cascade to the floor, Nalani lifted away the blue and red to reveal what lay below.

"Oh." Faran was rendered speechless for a moment. She would not have believed it possible, and she grinned to herself. Revealed was silk in a purple so deep that the shadowed areas appeared black.

"No one here can get close to such a colour even with cotton." Faran's voice held a note of awe and Nalani had an urge to speak, perhaps to say, 'not bad for a backward island people', but she refrained. He had never shown any such prejudice. She owed him some respect for that.

"Oh, we are going to be rich, Nalani my girl! We could ask an Emperor's ransom for such as this." He rubbed his hands together in glee.

"I thought that one might be popular," she said wryly. "It is difficult to obtain and apply this colour so it will need to be priced higher than the others."

"I have some of the richest clients in the city. It won't be a problem," he said, his usual jauntiness restored. "You said there were two new colours?"

"Sunset orange we call this one," she said, lifting a corner of the purple to reveal a rich, warm orange. "You said you had a customer asking for sun colours. I might get lemon yellow in the next consignment." She tilted her hand back and forth; it wasn't certain.

"Very nice." Faran grinned. "You have outdone yourself this time. Are you sure you won't marry me? I am a wealthy man and soon to be a great deal wealthier." His grin was infectious and though she had stiffened at his words – though she knew he only teased – she couldn't help a small laugh.

"I have money enough, Faran, and am in no hurry to marry anyone."

Faran gave a mock sigh and hurried to a locked door. Beyond it must be a room containing a safe. A clunk and the tinkle of a bell came from the shop beyond a curtained doorway at the same moment as Faran returned with two bulging bags.

"I could get my assistant to look after the shop and I could walk you home," he said, cocking his head to hear the quiet conversation from within the shop. "Just so you and those money bags get home safe, of course." His serious expression was spoiled by the playful glint in his dark eyes.

"I have been doing this for a few weeks and no one ever sees me. You are not coming to my residence." Her voice was firm.

"Ah well, can't fault a man for trying. Gods be with you." He again bowed theatrically.

"And to you. Until next time." Slipping the bags into the basket, Nalani left.

Nalani wended her way back through the bustling streets heading for home. Her basket was now much lighter, containing her bags of coins and the thin blanket that covered it. On one street a Priestess of Enara stood, mouth stretched wide and blessing passing citizens. They returned the smile and thanked her with gratitude. The Priestess posed in her deep blue gown, her oval face youthful under a tumble of black curls. Nalani did not make eye contact. These women, who were always young and beautiful, made her shoulder muscles tighten. She did not like them. They were dotted all over the city, mostly at crossroads or near the busiest buildings.

The quickest way home led her through the small square that lay before the humble temple to Gailean, the God of Storms. A few people were heading up the steps and through the always-open plain wooden doors. Many of them were wives of the fishermen out on the open seas to the north and west, praying for gentle seas and the safe return of their loved ones. Karas had a thriving harbour but the northern waters were notorious for sudden fierce storms that could take fishing boats and other trading vessels to the depths. For miles along the coast items were constantly washing ashore on the beaches. A few enterprising souls added to their coin by collecting this sorry flotsam. Nalani had come ashore four days south of Karas and missed any hint of such weather.

Within the square Nalani recognised a few familiar faces yet was still slightly taken aback when they gave her tentative nods and smiles. She almost forgot to return the smiles at first. However, her smiles grew easier and her step lighter. A shadowed gap existed between the Temple of Gailean and the tavern next door, ironically named 'The Calm Seas'. Garthwin hunkered in this gap. Garthwin was typical of the locals in appearance with olive skin, thick dark hair and dark eyes. There the similarities ended. He was the one vagrant to live away from the poorest quarters of town, as far as she knew. He had no air of gloom or despair about him; indeed, he seemed happy with his lot in life. Nalani admired his consistently cheerful and friendly demeanour despite his obvious hardships, and against her own guarded nature she was drawn to him, perhaps influenced by her first meeting with him. He sang one of his bawdy sea shanties in his cracked voice. One day she would ask him if he had been a fisherman in his unknown past. She strolled towards him.

"Morning, Nalani." He greeted her with a gap-toothed grin.

"Good morning, Garthwin," she replied and dug into a coin bag removing a few bright coins. His attention was claimed by the gleam of metal, though he made no move. She held her hand towards him.

"These are for you. Business has been brisk."

Hesitantly Garthwin reached out a grimy hand and swept up the silver coins. She knew enough not to hand over gold; he would never accept that. Nor would some tavern-keeps or shopkeepers feel obliged to give him the correct change, she was sure.

"You are too good to me." His voice had gone throaty and she feared he might cry. He hadn't so far; still she couldn't be sure.

"My family always taught me to give to those who have less, for one day the positions could be reversed."

He nodded, sniffed and wiped at his nose with his sleeve. "A family to be proud of. They all look like you?" he asked and took hold of her hand, placing it next to his. Through the dirt his olive skin was many shades lighter.

She began to respond when he grinned in delight.

"I shall have hot chocolate," he said, "with milk. In honour of you and your family with the beautiful skin." He began to stand up but sank down again with a disgruntled noise. "Once the tavern opens," he muttered.

"A little warm for hot chocolate, isn't it?"

"I don't care." His face settled into a stubborn cast. "I want to. I shall tell them it's for you," he added.

"Please don't mention my name," she said in alarm; visions of the attention this might bring her filling her with unease.

Garthwin tapped his nose. "Don't fret. I shall tell them it's in honour of my friend."

"Thank you." Nalani patted his arm. "You enjoy your hot chocolate. I must be getting home."

Garthwin waved goodbye in good humour, a hunched figure with his bundle of possessions beside him. This spot was the one he frequented most, for which Nalani would be forever grateful. He was the first person she had spoken to in this vast and confusing city. She had been overwhelmed by the size and the clamour and the sheer number of people. Everyone in a hurry to be somewhere. Everyone staring at her. She had no recollection of how she arrived in this part of Karas and she had stumbled towards the edge of the square, dazed.

"They've not seen your like before. They don't mean any harm though." A voice spoke from the shadows beside her. "Rare to see such dark skin and hair like mahogany. No wonder they're looking. Different and beautiful. It's more than some of these silly folks can take in."

Grateful for a friendly voice, she had found herself explaining her predicament. Garthwin had told her he knew the city 'backwards and forwards' and gave her clear directions to Faran's shop. On her return she sought him out once more and offered him some of the coin from the advance Faran gave her against the sale of her first silk delivery. He hadn't wanted to take it, but she insisted. That led him to suggest a place to stay. Now she felt they had an arrangement. She gave him coins and he would help her if she needed it. A satisfactory business arrangement.

Nalani entered Oleander Street still considering herself lucky to have found this place. The complete peace and emptiness during the day had initially been unnerving. She had to get used to the fact that at this time of day most residents were at work. Oleander bushes lined both sides of the street, the origin of the name. The clusters of pink blooms would give colour throughout the rest of summer.

She unlocked the shared front door three-quarters of the way along the street and ensured it clicked shut behind her. Sunlight fell through a large window, puddling on the tiled floor and casting illumination onto the three blue doors. Today no sound reached her from any of them. She rarely heard the elderly couple in the rooms at the back. They enjoyed a peaceful retirement now their children had taken over the running of their book-keeping business. The rooms opposite hers were a different matter. Such peace was rare and perhaps signalled that it would be brutally shattered later. There were three boisterous children and both parents worked. The woman's mother also lived there and attempted to take care of the children while both parents were out. She often struggled, completely out of her depth.

Nalani always knew when the father returned because a cloud of exotic aromas from his spice business always preceded him. She let herself into her own rooms. Could she expand her own business by selling him spices from home? They did not currently sell to anyone in Karas.

Nalani turned the key in her lock with a decisive twist and replaced the key in her pocket. She placed the basket on the floor and hung her cloak on the hook on the back of the door. The gentle yellow, blue, and green tones of the room soothed her, and she rested for a moment in the squashy armchair before the unlit fire. Karas was cooler than her home, though she doubted there would be many nights a fire would be needed. Her room was not large. It contained a relatively comfortable bed, made more comfortable by the new mattress she had purchased with her second payment from Faran, a small bookcase, a wardrobe, a table and two heavy lockboxes. The lockboxes had also been purchased with her second payment. She reached into the basket and took out the money bags and locked them into one of the boxes. Tomorrow she would take three of the bags when she met the next consignment of silk outside the city. The money paid for the silk and the week-long journey and what remained went back to her family. Perhaps there would be letters from home; there had been last time. She also needed to take some money into the city for safekeeping. Never keep it all in one place.

https://books2read.com/TheShard

About the Author

Jane Shand has always been an avid reader of fantasy and mystery and is an author of YA Fantasy.

She got hooked on fantasy after reading 'Lord of the Rings' at a young age and was determined to write books full of magic and adventure.

Her books always have magic, adventure, and some mystery. They are full of friendship and co-operation as well as danger and enemies. There will be a happy/satisfactory ending and some clean romance. Her books are all set in the same 'world' though on different continents and there is a thread/item that ties all the books together.

She lives in Hampshire, England with her family and two cheeky cats who would love to help her write.

Don't forget to use this link to claim your **Free** eBook **Origin of The Fallen** https://www.janeshandauthor.com/contact and sign up to Jane's email list.

Use https://www.twitter.com/JaneShand3
to follow Jane on Twitter
Use https://www.facebook.com/janeshandauthor/
to follow her on Facebook
Use https://www.goodreads.com/janeshand
to follow her on Goodreads
Use https://www.bookbub.com/authors/jane-shand
To follow her on Bookbub